THE JENNY

A New York Library detective novel

by

DAVID BEASLEY

*To Fran
all the best
David Beasley*

DAVUS PUBLISHING

DAVUS SUM/ NON OEDIPUS

FOR EUSTACE

Beasley, David R., 1931-

THE JENNY

ISBN 0-915317-03-6

I. Title.

PS8553.E14J46 1994   C813'.54   C94-900751-X
PR9199.3.B43J46 1994

Davus publishing

Canadian orders to
150 Norfolk St. S.,
Simcoe, Ont. N3Y 2W2
Canada

American orders to
P O Box 1101
Buffalo, N.Y. 14213-7101

ONE

My name is Rudyard Mack. I am with Security with the New York Public Library Central Building at the crossroads of 42nd Street and Fifth Avenue in New York City. Every morning, approaching this great edifice at the end of my walk to work, I think of it rising like a beacon of scholarship in a sea of hustling commerce and lost souls.

When I arrived before nine one morning, three cops were questioning the Assistant Business Manager who gave me the high sign over their shoulders to go to the boss's office at once.

As a Business Manager Sharkey Bugofsky was miscast in my opinion. I could see him as a Somoza, the aging dictator of a small third-world country, indulging his excesses. Bugofsky was in his best humor first thing in the morning and got progressively nastier during the day. By three in the afternoon, he was drunk. Dissipation had begun to show in his face despite his dark and rugged good looks. His body, which had the frame of an athlete, was in flabby decline. I thought of him as a disappointed, bitter man.

His secretary motioned me inside with her eyebrows. Bugofsky, barking over the telephone, glared at me.

"Got trouble, Rudyard," he said, slamming down the receiver. "We almost lost some postage stamps."

"The Miller Collection?" I was actually surprised that someone would try to steal from it.

Bugofsky related the facts of the attempted theft in angry staccato sentences with caustic asides about blacks making good runners but bad watchmen.

It seems that the night watchman had come from the blackness of the sixth-floor book stacks as the first glimmer of dawn pierced the tall windows of the Economics Division. As he entered the east reading room, he detected a whirring sound. He picked up his pace, strode to the next room and turned his flashlight at the glass-paneled offices under the windows overlooking Fifth Avenue. Silence. Suspicious, he unlocked the door to the hallway, closed it quietly behind him, and stepped carefully across the marble floor to the balcony overlooking the main entrance. The great window of the front caught the yellow light from the street lamps on Fifth Avenue. Through it, he looked down the deserted 41st Street in the dawn light of the eastern sky. Again he heard the sound but this time distinctly.

He descended the staircase, crossed the main floor, and peered up and down the long hallway. His flashlight caught the open door to the Comptroller's Office. Summoning his courage and keeping his light low, he moved swiftly to the door and peeked in. The sound of an electric drill assaulted his ears. He rushed part way down the room. A white man, crouching beside a small light at the end of the office, looked up, dropped his drill and reached threateningly into his coat pocket. The watchman fled. He loped down the hallway, through the iron gates, and leaped down a flight of stairs to the driveway of the inner courtyard and into the watchman's booth at the 40th Street entrance. He phoned the police.

1

He stayed in the booth and gaped nervously at the great door which was the only exit kept open throughout the night. Crouching in the booth, he was getting angry at the slowness of the police when he heard a car screech to a stop. He flicked a switch and the great door moved up. Two cops ducked under it. He ran out to meet them, crying, "He's in there!"

"Trouble was," Bugofsky sneered, "he wasn't in there."

The one hundred recessed glass panels near the Information Desk attracted scores of stamp aficionados who pulled them out and studied the stamps for hours. The intruder had intended to disconnect the alarm system by drilling into the wall behind the panels, taking away the backing to the cabinets and drawing them back into the privacy of the Comptroller's Office.

"He vanished," Bugofsky said, "but he left his drill behind."

"How'd he get in?"

"That's your problem, Rudyard. We also don't know how he got out, or if he got out. He might be here right now. He could step out from behind a bookcase during the day and walk out with the crowd." Bugofsky flashed a grin and then frowned. "You're the intellectual! You find out!"

"One guard isn't enough," I said, ignoring Bugofsky's little jibe.

"Tell that to Henry Betterton," Bugofsky growled. He raised his voice to a high pitch, "'The budget doesn't call for it.' That's what he'll tell you. So, Rudyard, catch this bastard before he strikes again."

This imperative was said in a tone of dismissal as Bugofsky began to leaf through the folders in front of him. I was wise not to ask another question. Stroking my hand pensively down the side of my face, I felt its leanness as a sort of reassurance and strode out of the office into the hunt.

The night watchman, who was waiting around to be dismissed by the police, gave me a clue. "He got red hair."

I inspected the stamp panels to see what the intruder was after. I recognized the Postmaster Provisionals. They were issued by the postmasters of a dozen cities between 1845 and 1847 when Congress authorized uniform postal rates but did not provide for stamp manufacture. The postmasters signed or initialed these make-shift stamps. The rest had no meaning for me, except for the prize of the collection, "the Inverted Jenny."

"Beautiful, isn't she," said a voice behind me.

I turned to look at a man of about thirty, slim with blue eyes and reddish hair. He held a notebook in one hand and was studiously noting down details of the stamps.

"What's beautiful about a plane flying upside down?" I asked to draw him out. I was curious about the special kind of obsession for stamps which I was told that all stamp collectors had to some degree.

"I mean the colors," he protested in a deep voice with a rough edge to it. "That deep carmine border and the heavenly blue center. Just fabulous! And its history is beautiful. I mean a stamp like that has an interesting history."

"What do you mean, history?" I smiled in disbelief.

"Are you a tourist?" he asked mockingly.

"No, I'm trying to learn." I looked intently serious.

"Well, that 24-cent stamp was one of a sheet printed in 1918 for Riggs Bank in Washington to commemorate a new airmail route. The Post Office didn't discover that the airmail plane came out upside down until after it gave the first sheet to a guy called Robey from the bank. It destroyed the others but couldn't get the first sheet back. Robey sold it to a Philadelphia syndicate for $15,000. It was broken up and the stamps were sold individually. By 1939 each stamp was worth $4,000."

"How much today?" I nodded in wonderment.

The man rounded his eyes in good humor. "You guess," he said. "Look here." He pulled out the next panel. "These inverted centers of 1869 are beautifully designed and printed, but Columbus is landing in America upside down. In 1939, this 15-cent dark-blue and red-brown was worth 2,000 used and 10,000 unused. It's worth four times as much now. These stamps over here, this 1909 bunch, they're called star plates because a star was added to the imprint to help divide them, the perforations being bad. In 1910 the watermark on U.S. stamps changed from the old double-lined letters to small single-lined letters. So stamps with the old watermark and the new starred plates were issued for only one year. So, you see, these 5-cent perforated stamps could bring up to 80,000 bucks." His enthusiasm was contagious, but he seemed as keen about their market value as for their characteristics as stamps.

"How do you know all this?" I asked innocently.

"I'm a keen amateur," the man smiled broadly. "Besides, do you know somebody tried to steal them last night?"

I stepped back in surprise. "What paper do you work for?"

The man laughed shortly. "I'm not a reporter. I just want to get a last look at these before they go off public view." He moved away.

Pretending to survey the area of the cabinets, I stood back, took out my pocket camera surreptitiously and snapped the redhead from the side. This was one more picture to add to my rogue's gallery of mug shots of visitors, readers, staff members. I was about to engage the garrulous stranger with another question when the librarian at the Information Desk called me. She held out the telephone receiver and whispered, "It's Mr. Bugofsky."

Bugofsky's voice sounded hysterically high. "Get up to the main reading room. An encyclopedia is missing. Christ! a whole goddamn encyclopedia. If it's a fifty volume set, I'm going to tell Betterton to shove it! We need manpower. And listen! I want a report on how that guy got into the building on my desk tomorrow morning!" He slammed down the receiver.

How could a thief know his way around a building the size of two city blocks with a maze of corridors and back staircases that would confuse the Cretan Minotaur and expect to disappear with the postage stamps? And how could a guy walk out past the guard with a multi-volumed encyclopedia? They must have been inside jobs. That would be the rational conclusion, but after twenty years with the New York Public Library I was prepared for anything irrational.

I took the wide staircase on the south side of the building that passed by work areas barred to the public. I stopped off on the mezzanine to watch technical assistants sitting at desks piled high with books and standing at catalogs checking bibliographies or answering one of the telephones to verify

3

bibliographic entries for reference librarians waiting on the public in some distant reading room. I like the staff to notice my presence for security reasons, but this day the workers were too busy to look up.

On the second floor, I circled through the serial cataloging room where catalogers stared at monitor screens and went into stack Six and down the center aisle between the book ranges which ran the length of the building. There were seven stacks and a cellar, altogether more than eighty miles of books. Maintenance workers swabbed the marble floors of the stacks regularly under the mistaken impression they were keeping the mice population in check.

I went up the stack staircase on the south-west side that overlooked Bryant Park and stepped into the far end of the South Reading Hall. Readers sat at long tables, huddled over books which they held under table lamps or leaned back in their chairs to catch the daylight from the great windows running high up both walls and from the light from the huge chandeliers.

In the partition area between the South and North Reading Halls, pages pushed book trucks off the stack elevator and pulled trays of books off the dumb-waiter that constantly brought books from all stack levels to this distribution point. The indicator board was lit up with numbers signaling to the waiting readers that their books had arrived from the depths.

I went to the librarian sitting at the reference desk and asked where the missing volumes of the encyclopedia had been shelved. The young man recognized me with a baleful look, led me several yards along the wall shelves and pointed to a vacant area on a lower shelf.

"Whoever carried them away," he said, pausing for emphasis, "must have got a hernia," and he returned to his desk.

The distance between the vacant shelf and the stack elevator was about thirty paces. The thief could have carried the volumes on a book truck.

I walked into the Catalog Room, nodded to the door guard and noted that readers were lined up waiting to speak to the librarians. I walked through the marble rotunda with its colorful frescos. Glancing both ways along the third floor hallway, as if half-decided to visit one of the special subject divisions, I suddenly wheeled and took the staircase on my left down to the second floor. I looked over the balustrade at the area below and stared out the great windows down 41st Street as the guard had done on the night of the attempted theft.

To my right were administrative offices and the Trustees Room, to my left the Economics Division. Behind me ran a corridor to the Slavonic and Oriental Divisions, at the end of which was a door to the stacks. Could the thief have come from the stacks through that door into the front of the building? Then he could have run down the stairway to the first floor and entered the Comptroller's Office by picking the door lock.

I descended to the first floor and looked along the corridor. In one direction lay the Periodicals Room, its windows barred; in the other lay the Map and Science Divisions with barred windows, which, of course, could be sawed through by some determined denizen of the underworld. I decided to check every single window on the first and basement floors and on the first and second floor stacks. It would take me hours, but if I did not do it, Bugofsky would be certain to ask me whether I had.

4

"Rudyard, my good man!"

I turned to see a heavy-set, white-haired gentleman who was a best-selling author of biographies standing by the door of the Allen Room. "I seem to have forgotten my key. Can you oblige?"

"Certainly, sir." I quickly stepped over to unlock the door with a pass key.

"Getting absent-minded," he said, "but, never mind, I've about another week of this grind and then I'm off to the Caribbean. Oh say, we're all of us sorry about the attempted stamp theft. Hang onto them, Rudyard." He smiled genially and closed the door as if eager to get on with his epic.

I thought at first that the privilege of a separate room for professional writers was at odds with the public mission of the Library, but then I thought it practical for writers who worked for months on end. The room was almost out of sight, behind the stamp cases and the metal paneling of the Personnel Offices filling the back part of the first floor. Besides, I liked the idea that some of the best brains of the nation worked together in one room on their future masterpieces. The very thought of it compensated for the dreary time I had to spend with Bugofsky.

I filled out a work order to move the stamps off the public display. As usual, no action was taken on the order right away so that two days later, when I awakened to my ringing telephone at 5 a.m., the stamps were still on display.

"Mack!" Bugofsky's voice rang out cold sober in my ear. "Some son of a bitch smashed the stamp panels and stole hundreds of thousands of dollars worth."

"All one hundred panels?" I gasped.

"No!" Bugofsky cried in irritation. "Only ten of them. The guard coming on duty at five heard the alarm and found the damage." Bugofsky's voice rose with vicarious excitement. "The night guard was doing his rounds in the stacks and heard nothing--not even the goddamn alarm. We've got a real one on our hands this time. Get over here now!"

Before I could answer, Bugofsky shouted, "For a measly 15,000 a year we could've got another watchman. We're meeting Betterton at seven. I want you to tell him that!" He laughed sarcastically. "It'll make the first page of the Metropolitan Section."

TWO

Henry Betterton stood at the far end of the Trustees Room with the white light of the early morning in the great windows behind him. I walked behind Bugofsky to a long table at which thirty or so trustees held their monthly meetings. This was where the powerful of the nation met. I felt uneasy in this room.

Betterton was tall, gray-haired, long-jawed, broad-shouldered--built like a football player, I thought. A director of several large companies, he had owned a football team and still contributed money to various sports. He also taught courses on minor English writers at Fordham University night school and offered a poetry prize in his name. As chairman of the trustees' subcommittee on library

5

security, he directly supervised Sharkey Bugofsky and his Department of Building and Maintenance Operations, known around the Library as the BM&O.

His smooth gestures were athletic; he had an aggressive, wide-awake stance as if he were waiting for a pitch or a lateral pass. I felt inferior to him because, by contrast, I was slightly built and at five foot nine I had to look up at him. And our backgrounds were so different since I had struggled up from poverty and lacked his education. Yet I sensed that he respected me, though he hardly knew me apart from the occasions I conducted public book discussions that he attended.

"Good morning, gentlemen," Betterton said in a friendly yet austere tone. He motioned us to sit at the head of the long table.

Bugofsky's hoarse accents clashed with Betterton's rich-toned voice. "I brought Mr. Mack. He's Director of Detection Operations. You remember."

"I recall very well indeed," Betterton smiled. "How long have you been in this position now, Mr. Mack?"

"Two years, sir." I wondered whether my lack of experience might be questioned.

"Like it better than Special Investigator, do you?" He eyed me humorously.

"More challenging," I said.

"Better pay, too," Bugofsky added with a short laugh.

"I've read your report on the first attempt, Mr. Mack," Betterton said frowning. "I have questions. Ah!" He looked at two men approaching through a side door that led from the executive offices.

Amos Anders, the Library Director, a gangling man in his early sixties, towered over the plump Edward Stavoris, the new Library President, recently retired as Chief Executive Officer of the Coca Cola Company.

"We read your report with interest, Mr. Mack," Stavoris said as they sat down. Stavoris had a reputation for making every minute count. His sharp nose and beady eye indicated a penchant for detail. "You assume a staff member left a cellar door open for the thief. But when you checked the doors, they were locked."

Betterton chipped in. "Someone could have locked the door from the inside before Mr. Mack checked." He turned to Bugofsky. "Did you have the doors checked first thing this morning?"

"The guard said they were tightly bolted," Bugofsky smiled indulgently. "We'll have to come up with another theory."

"Now, you mention meeting a redheaded man who knew a lot about stamps," Betterton, frowning, said to me. "How do you suppose that he knew that the robbery had been attempted?"

"The news had spread all over the building," Bugofsky interjected. "Any librarian could have told him."

"Just as important, sir," I said, feeling more comfortable now that Betterton seemed annoyed with Bugofsky, "how did this morning's thief know that more security had not been provided?"

"That's right!" Stavoris said emphatically and made a slight punching gesture. "This time he made a frontal attack with no concern for the noise he made."

6

"Presuming he was the same man," Amos Anders volunteered laconically.

"Amos," Stavoris nodded toward the hallway. "Talk to the reporters and emphasize that the Police Department is handling all the details."

Anders blushed slightly, nodded with a half-smile and departed for the hall.

"The press will want to know why we didn't beef up the security," Bugofsky complained to Betterton.

Betterton looked uneasily at Stavoris. "We'll talk about that another time," he said. "More importantly, the thief must have known that we intended to take the stamps off public view. That would account for his return visit so soon."

"Then the question is," Stavoris growled, "why weren't those stamps put away safely right after the first attempt?"

"Takes time," Bugofsky explained with an ingratiating smile. "It takes a number of men to handle those big glass panels."

Stavoris shook his head. "You get those cases dismantled this morning. I want the remainder of the stamps put in the Library safe until we know what to do with them. Mr. Mack! You report directly to Mr. Betterton on your progress until further notice. That will be all."

As I followed Bugofsky out of the room, I heard Stavoris mumbling to Betterton about the inefficiency in non-profit institutions.

"Quite a pair, right, Rudyard?" Bugofsky muttered.

I nodded. "They didn't say what stamps are missing."

"They don't care about the stamps," Bugofsky made a deprecatory gesture. "They care about money. The stamps are our worry. I have a librarian typing up a description for me now, but I know we lost the Inverted Jenny and Postmaster Provisionals."

"They ought to be hard to get rid of in the market," I said.

"You need only one buyer," Bugofsky growled as we reached the Business Office. "Get moving, Rudyard. Your job's on the line." He beckoned to his secretary to follow him to the inside room.

I stood in the hallway. I felt suddenly nauseous. Chasing down books stolen by readers was one thing, but messing with the underground market of stolen stamps was quite another. A library tour of a half-dozen visitors stopped near me. The tour guide patted the Oriental Division Book Catalog. "A good research library can give you the answer to anything," she announced impressively.

I sighed and headed for the Division of General Research where I began to look for the answer in the card catalog. "Philately, See Stamp Collecting." I flipped through the cards in the catalog and found a few promising titles. When I went to file the slips at the Enquiry Desk, I noticed Homer Margin, Chief Librarian, regarding me suspiciously over the backs of his hard-working librarians.

I nodded pleasantly. Homer, a short, severe-looking man wearing large glasses, stepped through the swing gate, took me by the elbow and led me to a near-by table.

"Did you see this morning's paper?" he asked. "It reports that you may have talked to the thief, a redheaded man who spoke about stamps." He spoke peremptorily, as if he were about to reprimand me.

"He could have been the thief," I agreed.

"But what a bold one! What accent did he have?"

I shrugged. "New York accent. Could have come from the Bronx."

"We'll watch for him," Homer said loftily.

I had a vision of innocent readers with Bronx accents being apprehended by Homer Margin.

"You can do something for me," I said. "I'm ordering up three books on stamp collecting. After I get the books, will you check back through the old request slips? I want to see who read them."

"We keep slips for five years," Homer winced.

"Just for the last year," I smiled. "I don't want more than I can handle."

Homer stepped back through the gates. "You just let me know what you want," he said meaningfully.

I filed my slips, looked at the number on the ticket given me by the clerk, and proceeded to the light indicator board in the North Hall. A guard at the door of the reading rooms was inspecting books that a reader was taking to the photocopying room. I tapped him on the shoulder to let him know that I was around. I surveyed the readers in the North Hall. Potentially, all of them were thieves. I walked down the center aisle and looked both ways along the reading tables. I recognized a gaunt-looking man who had been caught cutting up books with a razor blade. At the moment he seemed to be really reading, but was he not banned from the building? I stopped at the librarian's desk and called the Security Office to check him out. Sure enough, he was still under the ban. I instructed a guard to quietly lead him out of the building. At that moment my ticket number flashed on the board. I took possession of the books with pleasure, anticipating enlightenment, in this case about 1869 inverted centers, starred plates, the intaglio process and other arcane information necessary for catching a thief. Asking the clerk to turn my request slips over to Homer Margin, I settled down for a good read.

Forty-five minutes later I sensed Homer standing behind me.

"I've gone through the back files and pulled out the request slips for the books you have," Homer said stepping forward. "About fifty in all. Most were for the book you're reading now." He set a pile of library request slips on the desk.

"Did you notice anything unusual?" I asked leafing through them.

"I hate to say it," Homer said eagerly, "but a staff member from the Science Division called for the books several times. Do you see?" he pointed to a slip. "Edgar Berney, Room 121."

"Tall and thin," I said half-questioningly. "Light-skinned black. Not a librarian."

"A technical assistant," Homer replied disdainfully indicating that he considered it an inferior status.

"Xerox copies of these slips, please." I stood up. "And don't talk about this."

Homer looked offended that I thought it necessary to caution him. He scooped up the slips and walked away in a huff.

8

Before I talked to Berney, I had to establish a personal motive for Berney's involvement in the theft. The general motive, of course, was the common desire to hold gold bars, rare coins, oil paintings, stamps or whatever preserved value in these days of the inflationary dollar. Descending the stairway to the first floor, I went into the Personnel Office and asked for Berney's file.

Berney was 29, a "fair" worker, just good enough not to be fired for incompetence. Although his service reviews did not say it, I could see that the man was bright but badly motivated. Under "Hobbies" on his application form, Berney had written "stamp collecting." I began to picture the tall and diffident Berney who, I remembered, had a slightly hooked nose when I heard a shout for help. I dashed back to the hallway and saw the librarian at the Information Desk pointing down the hall. The guard at the Fifth Avenue entrance looked worriedly at me. I waved for him to stay at his post and ran towards the shouting. A husky young man, probably a student, pressed the full length of his body over an Hispanic struggling on the floor.

"He's got a knife!" the young man gasped.

I whipped out handcuffs, pressed my knee into the Hispanic's neck and got the cuffs on him. "Tried to rob you?" I asked the student, who looked shaken.

"Yeah...comin' off the elevator."

The thief, looking sourly at me as if I were in the wrong for stopping him, got to his feet slowly.

"Come to the office," I said to the student who was picking up a strewn notebook. "I'll need a statement." I shoved my prisoner ahead of me and scooped up a thin-bladed knife from the floor. I noticed Edgar Berney, tall and thin, in the small crowd outside the Science Division.

"I...I...I saw him pull the knife," Berney stuttered.

"Great!" I said. "I'll talk to you later."

THREE

The police took away the thief. I made a short report on the happening and added a note in the Department's book of statistics. It was the tenth attempted robbery with a knife within the year. Considering the size of the Library, the thousands of readers using it every day, and the riff-raff all around it in central New York, the statistics were modest. Just three attempted rapes so far. Plenty of purse-snatching, of course.

I reached for an envelope in the in-tray. It was from the lab technician giving me the bad news that my snapshot of the redheaded stamp aficionado had not turned out; it was a fuzzy gray showing only the shape of his head. What went wrong? Had someone tampered with the film?

I opened another envelope. It was Bugofsky's cryptic report on the findings by the police. They could not trace the purchaser of the electric drill used in the first attempt. There were no fingerprints. The glass panels had been smashed by a monkey wrench found in a corner of the hallway. The wrench came from the carpenter's shop in the cellar. The cellar, formed from the base of the reservoir,

9

which supplied the City's water in the last century, was a puzzle of corridors and rooms within rooms; only someone familiar with it could find his way.

I wished I could question the detective working on the case, but the police would rebuff any attempt by me to contact them. They didn't want interference, particularly from a library detective whom they regarded as little better than a doorkeeper. I had to depend on Bugofsky's reports for scraps of information about the police investigation. Likewise, Bugofsky had to depend on Henry Betterton because the police spoke only to Betterton.

Bugofsky had enclosed a typed sheet enumerating the stamps that were stolen. I noted that they amounted to 155 stamps, including four blocks of the 1909 issue in four, five, six and eight-cent denominations valued at $80,000. Why, I wondered, had the thief left ninety of the one hundred panels untouched? Had he been frightened off by the approach of the watchman? Or was he interested only in certain stamps? say, the Inverted Jenny or the 1869 inverted centers? Maybe he took the others just for extras, or to make it look as if the Inverted Jenny were not the sole object of the theft? Maybe the redheaded aficionado had been a plant whose purpose was to mislead me into thinking that the thief placed just as much value on the other stamps. Maybe the theft was committed by a philatelist with a fixation on the Inverted Jenny.

My telephone rang.

"Mr. Mack, I've located two volumes of the twelve of our missing encyclopedia," Homer announced proudly in an excited voice. "They were left on the second floor of the stacks."

"Very good," I said encouragingly. "The rest may be in the stacks too."

"If they are," Homer said, anger creeping into his voice, "I'll find the page who put them there."

I smiled to myself as I pictured Homer in the role of High Executioner. "What are you doing about the request slips?"

"Oh those!" Homer said as if it was old business, practically forgotten. "I've sent you xeroxes through inter-library mail. You know, I think you'll find it very strange that readers of those books gave addresses from all over the world. Places like Hong Kong."

"That is strange," I agreed. "Keep up the good work." I hung up.

I envisioned the case taking on international proportions. I was beginning to feel swamped with complications. A fear that the whole business was far beyond my capacities swept over me. I had heard through the grapevine that Amos Anders wanted to appoint a relative of his wife to my position. Bugofsky's secretary showed me a letter on the sly that told of the man's years of good work as a private detective and the insistence of Anders' wife that the Library employ him. I still had my job only because Bugofsky did not like Anders. But if I failed to make a good showing on this stamp case, even Bugofsky could not save me. The world of the unemployed was getting bigger and more savage every week. Men and women were looking through the trash baskets on street corners. I could see myself picking up a dirty crust of bread out of the rubbish. Of course, the library executives gave no sign that they expected me to solve the crime. After all, it fell under the jurisdiction of the Manhattan

Burglary Squad. But I sensed that my performance was being gauged. I stood up and with a faint heart set out to track down my first suspect.

As I took the 7th Avenue I.R.T. to West 110th Street to Edgar Berney's apartment, I calculated that Berney would be getting off work in a half-hour. The building looked dirty and run-down from the outside. The apartments were old railway flats, running narrowly from front to back. Berney's was on the first floor.

Berney had claimed his father as a dependent in his personnel records. I decided upon a direct approach and rang the bell. If the old man was not at home, I would wait for Berney. I heard the floor boards creek on the other side of the door and I sensed I was under inspection through the eyelet.

"I'm looking for Edgar Berney," I said.

"He ain't here," a voice croaked hoarsely.

"My name's Mack. I'm from the Library." I held up my detective I.D. card. "I'll wait for him." My voice carried the authority of the boss from the workplace.

The occupant hesitated, then began unlocking the locks. There were four distinct operations before the door opened revealing a thin old man with white hair and a white goatee. His eyes were red, and he smelt as if he had been drinking.

"Edgar ain't in trouble?" he asked as I stepped in.

I shook my head. "Just wanted to talk privately." I began walking toward the living room.

"Join me in a drink?" asked Berney senior.

"Sure," I said. "I'll have what you're drinking."

While the old man relocked the door and shuffled away to the kitchen, I passed what I sensed was Edgar Berney's bedroom and pushed open the door. It was an untidy room, the bed made badly, photographs and posters tacked helter-skelter over the walls. One photograph showed Berney in the company of young men leaning on the rail of a yacht named THE SYBIL. There was a mobile suspended from the ceiling--an abstract design that could have represented an aeroplane of the Wright Brothers' vintage. A touch of the artistic.

The living room was sparsely furnished: a worn couch, a comfortable reading chair with a lamp, a coffee table with a trunk area under the top, and a record player with a pile of records in one corner. Instinctively I scooped the magazines off the carved wooden coffee table and opened the top. Sure enough, stamp albums were there. I took them out, sat in a comfortable chair, and leafed through them.

Berney senior came slowly into the room. Eyeing me distrustfully, he gave me a glass of whisky.

"I heard Edgar collects stamps," I said returning the albums to the coffee table.

Berney senior sat on the couch with a sigh. "He's got more out back." He smiled with a wicked glint in his eye. "But he'll have to show them to you himself."

The old man obviously knew why I had come.

I raised my glass to him and acknowledged the return salute.

"Hope you catch that stamp thief," Berney senior said before he swallowed. "Edgar likes airplanes, I see," I said.

Berney senior guffawed. "You don't miss a thing." He took a long drink. "My son don't like 'em when they're upside down. Mind you, he wouldn't of minded havin' that Inverted Jenny that was stolen, but the only way he could get that is if it was given him."

"You trust Edgar, don't you," I said.

"Edgar's a good son. He supports me an' he don't complain. He's a good boy. Always bin honest. One hundred percent."

"I'll take your word for it." I wondered if I should try to see the stamps in the back room before Edgar arrived home.

"Say, Mack," Berney senior smiled suddenly. "That's your name, ain't it? Ain't you got Negro blood?"

Startled, I smiled. "What makes you think that?"

"You're a white man, but it's your eyes. Your eyes don't belong to a white man."

I nodded. "There's some African ancestors back there somewhere."

"Well, you can't be all bad then," Berney senior laughed.

I regarded the old man with good humor. I had underrated him. The old man was smart by trying to put me on the defensive.

The telephone rang. Berney senior still chuckling picked it up in the hallway. "All right, son. Your dinner will be waitin'. Say, there's a friend of yours here." He beckoned to me. "The library detective."

I took the telephone from him. Edgar had been asked to play chess after work so he was informing his father to expect him late. "Enjoy yourself," I said. "I'll get that statement about the fracas outside the Science Division from you tomorrow at work." I hung up.

"He witnessed a knife attack," I told Berney senior. "That's why I came to see him."

"Uh huh," the old man nodded and stroked his white goatee. "You want to see the rest of his stamp collection? I'll show it to you."

"Nope," I said and moved to the door. "Thanks for the drink."

Berney senior unlocked the door. "Say," he said, "Edgar hangs aroun' a lot a' stamp clubs and things like that. I'll tell him if he hears anythin' to let you know."

I walked down the dark hallway and felt further away from the solution than when I began, except for one thing. That mobile kept coming into my mind. It gave me the sensation of an early airmail plane in full flight. And there was another thing that I filed away as a minor mental note: all the photographs tacked to Berney's wall were of men.

FOUR

My apartment in the Gramercy Park area was not a Gramercy Park address, of course, but on Third Avenue close enough so that I could walk around the Park and consider it my backyard. My ex-wife and child lived in Los Angeles.

They had stormed out of my life years ago never to be heard of again. Money was what they wanted and what I seemed unable to provide. My fault was in my caution. I was uncomfortable taking risks, which, I thought, accounted for my long service in a stable institution like the Library. The bad experience of my marriage had made me even more cautious. Although I felt lonely at times, I feared getting close to another woman. My days of romance were over, I thought. In the evenings I did my own cooking, read historical narratives, and watched television.

This evening, however, I had a sudden desire to eat out and to be in the company of others. I turned into a select bar-restaurant on Third Avenue and sat at the far end of the eating area. I ordered fish and beer. Most of the tables were occupied. Suddenly, I noticed with a start that Detective Buckle, who had been assigned to the stamp theft case, was sitting at the bar with a slim, redheaded man who looked like the stamp aficionado I had spoken to on the morning after the foiled first attempt on the Miller Collection. The heavy-set Buckle was listening with a serious mien and writing in a notebook as the redhead talked. Cautiously taking out my camera and adjusting it for the lighting, I snapped their picture.

I was distracted by the arrival of my fish and the waitress's questions about sauce and dressing for my salad so that when I looked back at the bar the men had gone. The incident mystified me. Was the redhead involved in the crime and cooperating with the police? Or had he been a police decoy planted at the scene of the crime on the assumption that the thief would return? I sensed that the redhead was a fraud and had intended to mislead me. But I didn't know why. And now that I saw him with Detective Buckle, I began to doubt my own assumptions. I wondered whether they had seen me enter the restaurant, and whether that was why they had gone so suddenly. I began feeling like an outsider in this case. I sensed that if I let this feeling prevail, it would be like a mysterious sea monster swallowing me whole and suffocating me in the darkness of its belly. I needed action to keep from dwelling on uncertainty.

My dealings with the New York City Police Department were confined to turning over petty criminals apprehended in the Library to police officers who would pick them up and let most of them go with a warning. I knew that Detective Buckle had a good arrest record and had been involved in solving some murders that had caught the newspaper headlines. But I was leery of Buckle in the same way that New Yorkers were leery generally of their police. One could never be sure which party a policeman would believe. The line between accuser and accused had become a very fine one for the police because some of them had a vested interest in criminal activity such as drug-selling, extortion, and protection racketeering. Moreover, the police were political in a parochial way. They gauged the importance and influence of both sides in a dispute before deciding how to deal with it. The New York Public Library still kept its respect as an institution, but the world of books and scholarship was regarded disdainfully as quaint and weak. I thought I saw hints of this disdain in Buckle's attitude to the stamp theft and to me in particular. With sudden anger, I bolted down the rest of my meal while I swore to prove the worth of the Library and myself to that cynical and skeptical world whose reading never went further than the tabloids.

As I walked along Third Avenue and watched the traffic stream one-way uptown in the waning light of early evening, I felt a need for human contact, some sort of honest contact. I had no woman; hadn't had one for a year. On impulse I hailed a cab and went to an old short building squeezed between taller ones on West 43rd. The street door was open. I walked up the stairs to the fourth floor and rapped at the big tin door under a sign that said "New York Library Guild." I was lucky. A woman's voice asked who it was and, satisfied, that it was me, let me in.

"Come to the back room," she said. "I'm doing some work."

Arbuthnott Vine was politically a leftist but not a member of a political party as far as I could determine. I distrusted leftists in general but liked some of them in particular. Arbie Vine, as she was called, was an idealist who really believed the world could be changed. I trusted her as a human being but not as a political being. She was in her thirties, with long dirty brown hair, blue eyes, slim, high-breasted and sort of girl-scoutish in her actions.

"You're working late," I said, following her to a small room where there was a large desk strewn with papers, some chairs, and vertical files.

"Had a committee meeting," Arbie explained, "but half the fuckers didn't show so I threw those who showed out of here early."

"That's expected," I said sitting in a hard chair. "Your members don't care about politics; they want money."

"You know and I know they won't get more money until they change the system," Arbie plopped down behind the desk and threw her leg over one corner of it. "What's on your mind, detective?" she smiled winsomely.

"You might be able to shed some light on a problem," I said feeling foolish because it seemed unlikely that she could help. "It's got me stymied."

She laughed. "Come out with it, Rudy. You're the only guy in management who can talk straight, you know."

"Well, it's this stamp theft. It's getting me down. I think it was an inside job but there's so many outside possibilities, I'm getting confused."

"Oh, it was an inside job alright," Arbie said. "Probably one of the maintenance men was in on it, I don't know. But you know my philosophy-- nine times out of ten if there's any fishy business in the Library, management's got to be involved."

I made a pained expression.

"No!" Arbie dropped her leg and leaned forward. "Stamp thefts don't really interest me; I mean, they can steal all the fuckin' books and rare prints they want, and I bet they've taken quite a pile over the years, and we'll never catch 'em because they got the control."

"Who's they? Are you talking about the trustees?"

"Yeah, I'm talking about the trustees. Look here." She leaned over her desk and unfolded a large piece of cardboard on which were sketched numerous circles interlinked by straight lines. "In each of these circles I've printed the name of a company. If you take all of the trustees and the companies of which they are directors, you get quite a nice pattern. You begin seeing how many times they meet one another in the course of a year. You see how their outside interests sort of impinge on their responsibilities as trustees of the public good. And if you look into their backgrounds," she picked up a sheet of paper, "like this guy, Shifter, who made his money in construction, you learn that the Securities and Exchange Commission convicted him for stock fraud. And if the SEC condemns you, you're really baddy-bad."

"What are you telling me, Arbie? That one of the trustees snuck into the building at night and stole the stamps?"

"Come on, don't play dumb!" she laughed. "You want a clue, don't you? I'm telling you where to look."

"You think I should find out what trustees have stamp collections?"

"I find a lot of answers to what's happening in the Library by looking at this chart," she frowned. "It's a goddamn shame but that's where we're at today."

"You'll get me fired," I smiled. I liked her because she had guts. She fought management on all issues without compromising especially when the big union leaders were already in management's pockets.

Her telephone rang and she snapped up the receiver. "Oh hi!" she said cheerily. I felt that I should excuse myself. She covered the mouthpiece. "It's your boss, Bugofsky," she giggled. "He's higher than a kite." She spoke sweetly into the receiver and rounded her eyes at me. "Lunch tomorrow? I'll call you tomorrow morning." She clamped her hand back on the mouthpiece. "Wants to discuss upcoming negotiations. He's really after my ass. It's all fantasy-- the drunken old bum." She removed her hand and spoke brusquely to Bugofsky. "Look, Sharkey dear, some one's just come into the office. I've gotta go." She put her hand back. "I won't call him, of course. He won't remember a thing tomorrow. But I can't get rid of him. Wait a minute, I've got an idea." She spoke to Bugofsky. "Tell me who stole the stamps and I'll meet you tomorrow. You know everything, so tell me." She laughed. "Amos Anders! Why, he wouldn't steal a library pencil. No deal, Sharkey baby!" She hung up. "You see, Rudy, you're the only guy who thinks management can do no wrong."

"I don't think the library director stole the stamps," I chuckled.

"Neither does Sharkey, but he hates Anders."

The telephone rang; she picked up the receiver, dropped it back, then took it off the hook.

"He's a persistent son-of-a-bitch. You must hate his guts."

I stood up to avoid discussing my feelings about Bugofsky. "You haven't really helped me very much."

"I really have," she said. "But you're too dumb to know it. You're welcome to see this chart anytime. Good luck, Rudy."

I waved and let myself out the door. It was dark when I reached the street. I felt the night-hum of New York, and took in the mix of bright lights and excitement which concealed the endless cries for help. I decided to walk home.

Arbie Vine might have been right. Somewhere in back of the theft was a rich collector who coveted those stamps, someone who was willing to pay handsomely to possess them. Or, it might have been someone who knew that the Library intended to take all the stamps off public display. Only the trustees, Bugofsky, the technicians fulfilling the work order, and I knew that. My natural

15

caution (what some would call conservatism) inclined me to doubt that line of reasoning. Nevertheless, it did disturb me.

On impulse, when I saw the great stone library lit up on the Fifth Avenue side, I mounted the steps, tapped the guard who was day-dreaming at the entrance, and climbed the steps to the third floor research room. Homer Margin was working late at the librarian's counter. Seeing me approach, he reached behind him and passed me an envelope furtively, as if it were contraband.

"Didn't know you worked nights," I said.

"When there's something big happening, I do," Homer said eagerly. "I'm trying to pick up what I can. I want those stamps back."

Homer liked to hide in the stacks to eavesdrop on the conversations of staff. I had stumbled on him many times crouched in dark areas. Many a page had been fired over the years for smooching when there was a lull in the demand for books.

"Heard anything?" I asked. I took the photocopied pages of the call-slips out of the envelope and scanned through them.

"Yes," Homer leaned forward and looked suspiciously at a young librarian standing at the information counter. "I was taking some papers to the Director's Office this afternoon, and I heard a terrible argument going on from the direction of the President's Office. On the excuse that I was looking for something, I went into his secretary's office. Luckily she wasn't there so I got right up to the door and heard practically everything they said."

"Oh yes?" I could see no pattern, no clues from the names on the call-slips. True, Edgar Berney had called for one of the books several times.

"The President was furious with Henry Betterton for the poor security arrangements," Homer continued. "I've never heard Mr. Stavoris so angry. But then Mr. Betterton hit back. He accused Mr. Stavoris of losing his cool because one of his companies had insured the stamps."

I was interested. "What did Stavoris say?"

"He accused Betterton of hitting below the belt, that his company would have to pay a lot, but his main worry was the other priceless stuff in the Library. Supposing, he said, the manuscript of Eliot's *Waste Land* was stolen from the Berg Collection. Could Betterton guarantee that it was safe? Mr. Betterton said the conversation was becoming impossible. I just had time to move to the secretary's desk and pick up some papers when he came steaming out of the office."

At that point, I came upon the name of "Stavoris" scribbled on a call-slip for the same book Berney had been reading. It was on the last sheet of photocopied slips and must have been filed almost a year ago.

"That's interesting," I said as I held Stavoris's name in front of me like a tarot card foretelling the future.

"Well, I thought it was," Homer said. "I don't think those men like each other."

I excused myself. I felt strangely captive as if fate were taking me in a direction of which my mind disapproved. I went to a telephone in the hallway and called Arbie.

"What do you want?" she demanded angrily.

16

"It's Rudy," I said.

"Oh," she laughed. "I thought it was your boss again." Her voice reassured me, calmed me.

"Will you look at your chart and tell me with what insurance company Stavoris is connected?" I thought I detected a slight tone of amusement in her ready agreement, but she left the phone for a moment and came back on the line sounding almost business-like.

"Continental Insurance," she said.

"Oh, oh," I said as if seeing a warning signal.

"Starting to move in my direction?" Arbie asked, letting her amusement come into her voice now. "Smart boy."

I had a big hunch but I would have to wait till tomorrow to check it out. Arbie's voice stayed with me as I went into the night. I sighed poignantly, certainly with regret. I was middle-aged, washed-up, and she was out of reach.

FIVE

Continental Insurance was in a new building on Madison Avenue in the Forties. I went there about ten in the morning after developing the film I had taken of Detective Buckle and the redheaded man. This time it turned out well. I had a good profile shot of the redhead. I had my own darkroom in my apartment. I wished I had developed the first shot I had taken of the redhead, but Bugofsky had wanted the lab to do it right away.

I stood in the lobby and watched the traffic getting in and off the elevators. When the porter finally took his break, I caught up to him at the door of the coffee shop. I showed him my detective I.D. and suggested we have coffee. The man was defensive at first, but when he saw the picture he became more agreeable.

"I don't know the fat guy," he said, referring to Detective Buckle, "but the other guy, this one here with the red hair, he works in this here building. I seen him plenty of times."

"Did you see him today?" I asked, trying to keep from looking excited.

The porter shook his head. "I don't see him for weeks. You could say he don't work regular here."

"Do you know his name?"

The porter shook his head again. "I know he works for Continental Insurance." He called to the waitress. "Margie, do you know this guy's name?"

Continental Insurance! My hunch was right! The redhead was working for Stavoris.

The waitress, a pretty girl, studied the snapshot. "I've seen him in here, but I don't know his name. Maybe Bill does." She went to the manager, a sharp-eyed Greek who took the picture from her and came over to us.

"This person on the left is Mr. Macdonald," the manager said looking suspiciously at me. "Why you want to know?"

"He's a library detective," the porter explained.

"What'd he do?" the manager said sardonically indicating the picture. "Didn't return his library books?"

"They're overdue a month," I said.

"Geez!" the manager laughed. "I was jokin', but you're serious. Hasn't your Library got better things to do?"

"Books are our business," I said taking back the snapshot.

"It's getting more like a police state every day," the manager complained.

I grinned, paid for two coffees and headed for the eleventh floor. The receptionist at Continental Insurance informed me that Mr. Macdonald worked out of their office in London, England; he had been here recently but had gone back.

I left my card and asked that Macdonald call me when he showed up again.

"He has red hair, hasn't he?" I asked as I turned to go.

"Very nice red hair," she smiled. "He's a good-looking man."

"He's the one I'm looking for," I said.

When I got back to the Library, I found the watchman who had encountered the thief on the first robbery attempt. Since that incident, he had been transferred to day duty and was monitoring an exhibit of prints on the second floor.

"Dunno," the guard said when he saw the photo. "Could be the man." He pressed his large black hand over his eyes as he tried to bring back the scene that night. "I flashed him full on, but all I remember was his red hair." He shook his head. "I don't think that I can recognize him. I was scared out of my mind."

"We'll talk again," I said. I walked to the other end of the hallway, past the sign reading "Staff Only," and stepped into the small outer office attached to the President's Office. It had been turned over temporarily to Henry Betterton who was sitting at his desk.

Betterton swept a box off the chair beside the desk to a shelf on the other side as if making a lateral pass. "Sit down. Got some news, Rudyard?"

"I've located the mystery man with the red hair. His name is Macdonald and he works for Continental Insurance which insured the stamps."

Betterton seemed thunderstruck. "Are you sure?"

"I'm sure he was the redhead who spoke to me about the stamps, but our watchman can't be sure he is the same redhead who made the first attempt to steal them."

"It makes sense," Betterton pondered, "that he would know about the stamps since he was the insurance appraiser."

I could see Betterton's mind trying to make a connection between President Stavoris, the insurance appraiser and the theft. He looked bewildered. I handed him the snapshot of Detective Buckle and the redhead. "This is for you. I made more prints."

Betterton frowned at what he saw. "So this is what he looks like, and Buckle knows him. This is getting interesting," he smiled. "The police don't want to tell us anything of what they're doing. Let's keep this information to ourselves, shall we?"

I nodded.

"I hope we can trust Buckle," Betterton said doubtfully.

18

"We haven't had a full-scale investigation into police corruption for at least five years," I said.

Betterton looked at me with humor. "Okay, Mr. Mack. I suppose we won't know more until you get in touch with this insurance appraiser."

"I have some other ideas," I said.

"Not now. Mr. Bugofsky wants to see you." Betterton returned to his papers.

As I headed for Bugofsky's office I considered it an important fact that Betterton knew nothing about Mr. Macdonald of Continental Insurance. I knew he would be taking a closer look at Mr. Stavoris.

Bugofsky kept me waiting until he finished with the representative of a big reprinting company. By giving this company the monopoly to reprint rare books from the Library's collection, Bugofsky got a share of the company's profits and perks such as free rides on its private airplanes. Sharkey was a shark when it came to making money in a non-profit institution.

"Where the hell you been, Rudyard?" Bugofsky growled. "You work for this department, you know, not for Betterton and those idiots! We got to find that missing encyclopedia. It's a very important reference work, and I'm getting a lot of flak about it. The librarians got to have it."

"There's a rash of thefts of encyclopedias from libraries all over the country," I said. "They're worth a lot now."

"Well, somebody got it out of the building, and I want you to find it right away," Bugofsky snarled for emphasis. "Get out of here, I got work to do." His hand went for his drawer where he kept his liquor and rested there while he waited for me to go.

My line of work was becoming more difficult. There was a time when books were stolen only by bibliophiles; their actions were so amateur that they could be located and apprehended without much trouble. Lately, the stealing of books had reached alarming proportions; in fact, to the point where I feared that organized crime was involved in a systematic theft of the nation's major libraries.

I took the freight elevator down to the second level stack where Homer Margin said that the two volumes of the encyclopedia had been found. I went to one of the windows ranged along the west side of the building overlooking Bryant Park and gauged that there was a fifteen-foot drop to the ground. The windows swung out so that it was possible for a man to lower the volumes to the ground and squeeze through the window and climb down. The thief could have gotten only four or five volumes at a time through the window. Could he have been interrupted before he had passed through all the volumes and had had to flee without the last two?

Poking my head out, I spotted a strand of wire leading from the sill of the next window to the ground. It was tied to a bar just outside the window. I untied it and drew it in. Exhibit No. One. Probably the wire had been used rather than a rope as it would not be noticed by someone standing in the park. It would have dropped the thief behind the bushes growing alongside the building. He could then proceed through the deserted park onto 42nd Street or the quieter 40th Street and into a waiting car. I stood at the window for a moment to watch a drug transaction in the park and wondered whether the stamp thief had escaped out the same window. It was possible that the stamp thief had entered by the 40th Street entrance into the stacks when the night watchman was making his rounds.

I rolled up the wire and walked the length of the second stack to the stairwell at the south side. These stairs led directly down to the 40th Street passageway. If the stamp thief and the encyclopedia thief were one and the same person, what connection was there between the two thefts? Were they done for the same employer or was the thief a freelancer? When I got back to my office, I set out instructions for the night watchmen. Each watchman was to check for the two volumes of the encyclopedia on the reading room shelves on every hourly round until further notice. Should they be missing, the watchmen were to notify me by the nearest telephone which was on the librarian's reference desk twenty yards away. During the hours that the library was open, the librarian on duty in the reference room was to make spot checks to see that the two volumes were on the shelves. I expected that these procedures would not have to be carried on for long.

SIX

The police got their first break in the case of the stamp theft. A stamp dealer in Buffalo, New York, reported that a client told him that he had seen an Inverted Jenny in the private collection of James New, a rich businessman in the area. I got the news from Henry Betterton.

"If it is our stamp," Betterton said with emphasis, "and we're not sure because we've located ninety-seven of the one hundred printed, and we don't know who has the remaining three, but if it is our stamp, Mr. New was most incautious in showing it to two or three of his close friends."

"What's the point of having it if you can't show it off?" I asked sardonically.

"At any rate, we're stymied until it can be positively identified," Betterton said. "And that may take some time, perhaps years, perhaps forever."

"I don't think I can pursue the case that long."

"Keep up your good work," Betterton drawled. "Anymore on the insurance angle?"

"Still working on it," I said. "It's simmering."

"I think that's our best approach," Betterton advised.

As I left Betterton's office, I felt I had an excuse to see Arbuthnott Vine. As luck would have it, I ran into her as she was coming out of the Personnel Office.

"Can we talk?" I asked. "There's been a break in the stamp theft."

"Sure, but I'm hungry," Arbie said looking at her watch. "Want to have lunch?"

"I don't trust the cops," she said ten minutes later, after I filled her in with the latest news, and as she picked at a chef's salad in a coffee shop on 39th Street. "They don't know their ass from a hole in the ground. This guy New could have bought the stamp legitimately."

"If you can get me the low-down on him," I said, "we'll see how legit he really is."

"I get all this horseshit for you," she said. "What do you do for me?"

"At your service." I swallowed some cheese omelet.

"How about some inside dope on Sharkey, like what he's going to ask the staff to give up in our negotiations?"

"Please don't ask me that," I groaned.

"I'm sorry," Arbie put her head down. "I was kidding." She looked up and smiled. "I'll join you for the pleasure of upholding justice against crime!" Her voice sounded husky and sexy.

"Management knows you are not the surrendering type anyway," I said.

Arbie raised her eyebrows. "What do you mean?"

"I mean," I said hurriedly, "that you won't give up any staff benefits."

Arbie looked amused and toyed with the straw in her Coca Cola. "How could I think that you could mean anything else."

I felt faintly uneasy. "I don't think anyone could get the better of you in a fight."

"Oh yes?" Arbie said suddenly. "I'm being hit from both sides at once. It's hard to tell if its library management or the big Union boys who hurt me more."

"I don't want to know about it," I said.

"I'm not going to tell you, but I'm warning you to start thinking about this comfortable system you feel so secure and snug in. Someday you're going to be taking the hits, and you're gonna say, 'Gee, why me? I've been minding my own business.' Okay, detective, I've got to go. I'll get a librarian in the Economics Division to work on James New. Call me in two days."

I watched her stride from the coffee shop. She was the modern-day Lancelot entering the fray in the cause of honor and justice whereas I was nothing but a snoop around the castle. I finished lunch and sauntered back to the library to snoop along the halls for undesirables, snoop on the library attendants, and snoop through the reading rooms for violators of library regulations.

When I called Arbie two days later, she asked me to come to her headquarters. "I've got some surprising news for you, my dear supporter of the bourgeoisie."

I found her in a dress and high heels. There was a delicious smell of perfume in the air as she led me to her office.

"Well!" she said sitting down with a thump. "Henry Betterton must know James New. There are at least three companies of which they are directors, and one of them is Rinehardts, the big publishing company!"

"What's significant about Rinehardts?"

"It publishes stamp albums!" she said excitedly.

I stared at her. "Do you really think Betterton is in on this theft? That's impossible!"

"Nothing's impossible when you're dealing with the enemy!" Arbie said. "You should concentrate on this connection and forget about redheaded men and Edgar Berney."

"I have forgotten about Edgar Berney," I said. "But didn't you tell me that New could have bought the Inverted Jenny? Weren't you the one who was accusing me of jumping to conclusions about James New, trying to pick on an innocent stamp collector to avoid accusing a library trustee?"

Arbie put her head back and laughed. "Okay, okay, we may be on a wild goose chase, but I think it's the best lead we've got."

"Lead?" I smiled. "I don't see any traces, any footprints."

"Let's suppose that Betterton arranged to have the stamps stolen for James New. He'd do it for one of two reasons: either he owed New something or he and New formed a partnership to profit from it."

"Wait!" I said looking at the chart of trustee directorships. "Maybe it's not Betterton. Maybe it's Stavoris. Stavoris is a director of one company that includes New on its board."

"What company?" Arbie took the chart from me.

"Kodak. Notice the monthly meetings are held at the headquarters in Rochester, not far from Buffalo, and a short flight from New York," I said pointedly.

"What's that supposed to mean?"

I shrugged.

"Are you making fun of me, you s.o.b.?" Arbie threw down the chart. "I'm not going to help you unless you take me seriously."

I laughed. "I'm sort of serious. Don't forget that Stavoris is a director of Continental Insurance which insured the stamps."

Arbie clasped her cheeks in her hands. "Oi vey! Complications!"

"I haven't dealt with anything like this before," I said. "It's one thing to catch staff members who steal from the library, but trustees! I think we could be imagining things."

"Look, detective, you always struck me as a good judge of character. Why do you draw the line at the trustees?"

I avoided her eyes.

"Because they pay your salary?" Arbie suggested.

"For one thing," I said, "I report to them, they take action on what I find. If they're both judge and criminal I won't get a conviction."

"My dear Rudyard," Arbie reached over to pat my hand. "If you were a socialist, you'd have more faith in the people. And don't give me that indulgent smile when you hear the word 'socialist.' It happens to be the one word that has brought true progress to the human race for the past two centuries," she glowered. "You should know more about your bosses; it might cure you of your obsession with capitalists. Our library president, Bill 'Have a Coke' Stavoris, worked his way up the corporate ladder by his ruthless treatment of workers. He came from a poor immigrant family that faced exploitation all its life--the same kind he made other families suffer after he proved that he belonged to the big boys. Sweet Amos Anders got his start as an intelligence officer in World War Two, then worked his way up through Army base libraries to marriage with a general's daughter and a plum job in NYPL because she wanted to live in New York. The third in that cosy triumvirate, big sport Henry Betterton, was born with a silver spoon in his mouth. Unlike the other two, he's never had to kiss anyone's ass. But that doesn't mean he can be trusted. I won't tell you about his business deals 'cause I'd shock a faithful capitalist prole like you."

I laughed. "I know they're not angels. But who is? Moreover, these associations, connections or whatever you want to call them, they're too vague. We'll have to wait for clues."

Arbie smiled sympathetically. "We'll wait for ideas," she said with an understanding tone. "Why don't you relax for a change and come with me to a play tonight?" When she saw my surprise, she added quickly. "Like the Greek in the bathtub you might get an idea."

"Eureka!" I said.

"My girlfriend just called me and can't come, so I've got an extra ticket. Besides, I hate going alone."

"Fine," I said. "So long as it's not Shakespeare." Actually, if it were Shakespeare I would have accepted with joy. "I'll pick you up for dinner."

"No, meet me at the City University cafeteria after six," she said. "I have a grievance hearing and I may be late, so start eating."

The City University Graduate Center was on 42nd Street across from the Library. I stood by the bar and drank white wine until 6.30 when Arbie charged off the elevator, waved her satchel, and called me into the cafeteria.

"I told you to eat," she said. "Don't play the gentleman with me."

"There's plenty of time," I said.

"Only because we're eating cafeteria style." Arbie searched the counter for food she wanted. "I'm bloody mad, anyway. I mean, I'm goddamn upset. This grievance I'm handling should have been resolved at the second step, and here I am taking it to the Director who plays the same little dumb game as all the other supervisors. I think management wants to break our treasury by forcing everything into arbitration."

"That's just to give you a failure complex," I said. "It's called wearing you down."

"I've got plenty of energy," she said, "but it's the grievants I feel sorry for. You know, Rudy, I hate those smug management bastards!"

"Don't get emotionally involved," I warned. "It's a business to them. You can't change anything."

"Sure as hell I'm emotionally involved. I wouldn't be a union leader otherwise," she glared at me. "I'm not like one of those big union shits making the deals downtown."

I regarded her as she ate. I felt a tenderness for her because she was vulnerable and prepared to take the consequences.

"I'm glad you're on my side," I said.

"Yeah, well, hurry up and eat your food or I'm going to the play without you."

The play was an Off-Broadway production--far out by my standards but engrossing nevertheless. Moreover, it was the offstage action that really mattered. About half-way through the first act we held hands. During the intermission we regarded each other with a new interest, or perhaps it was an old interest that had gone unrecognized until then. We spoke more animatedly, laughed more than usual. We thought the play was excellent. We held hands through the second act, and it felt more natural.

I took her for a drink. The table lantern made private our table with a glow that seemed to set us apart from the others. I suddenly leaned over and kissed her, and she kissed me back. The waitress approached to ask if we would like anything more. I paid, and we left for my apartment.

I felt an immense relief as I took her naked into my arms. It had been so long. I needed her emotionally, and she sensed it. It didn't matter that my performance was poor. Somehow the emotion overcame me. Arbie laughed teasingly. She called me the hard-boiled detective with a soft spot.

Shortly after three in the morning, we awoke to my ringing telephone. I had to reach over Arbie to pick up the receiver. An incipient sense of guilt made me wonder if someone were calling me to account for bedding this young lady.

It was the Library night watchman. The two volumes of *Baker's Encyclopedia* were gone! Instantly awake, I informed a drowsy Arbie of its importance while I dressed.

"I'm coming with you!" she said.

"No!" I said. "You might get hurt."

"Well, so might you!" she said throwing off the sheet and making me suddenly wish we were going back to bed.

She dressed as quickly as I did so that, within minutes, we were in the street hailing a cab and speeding the twenty odd blocks to the 40th Street side of the Library.

Bryant Park was pitch black with the street lamps sending incursive rays of light onto its perimeters.

"Stay in the taxi," I ordered Arbie.

"No, I'm coming with you," she said.

"This guy could be a killer," I shouted. "In fact there could be half a dozen killers in that park right now."

"I'm coming with you," Arbie said.

Sighing, I told her to stay close. Entering the park just behind the Library building, I paused until my eyes became accustomed to seeing in reduced light. I tread swiftly to a columned portico-like edifice harboring the statue of William Cullen Bryant and erected in the days when Americans honored literati. I stood for a moment surveying the back of the building.

"Do you see that window on the second floor level?" I whispered and pointed it out to Arbie. "Do you see any movement?"

"I think I see a rope being let down," she said.

I grunted. "You stay here and watch." I glanced round at the park benches and near-by bushes to see that there were no derelicts lying about. "If anything happens to me, get back to the taxi and get help."

"Be careful," she said.

I crept up to the bushes by the library wall and waited. Presently a man appeared at the window. He was tall and thin and just fitted through the window opening. He had a bag slung over his shoulders. He carefully lowered himself down the wall by the rope. I recognized Edgar Berney.

When Berney was close enough to the ground to jump, I stood up and stepped forward to seize him. Suddenly pushing out from the wall Berney shot

24

out his legs and kicked me flat onto my back into the bushes. Berney jumped to the ground and ran.

Scratched and furious, I rolled onto my feet and gave chase, but the fleet Berney was already on the stone patio and streaking for a complete getaway onto 40th Street. It was then that a figure threw itself on Berney and knocked him to the ground. Like a wildcat, Arbie clung to the bag around Berney's shoulders. The hapless Berney, regaining his feet and seeing me approach, threw the strap off his shoulder and ran without the bag into the grassy center of the park.

"Come back, Edgar!" I shouted into the darkness. "I know who you are, you can't escape!"

I lifted Arbie to her feet. "Good work!" I took the bag and felt in it. "The encyclopedia," I said. "Come back, Edgar! It'll be bad for you if you don't."

I tried to help Arbie brush the dirt off her slacks. "Are you all right?"

"The best tackle I ever made," she said.

"Let's get out of here." I took her by the arm and hurried to the exit onto 40th Street. "We're sitting ducks for the muggers who sleep here."

"What are you going to do about Berney?" Arbie asked as we reached the waiting taxi.

"Nothing," I smiled, "except to find out where the rest of the encyclopedia is." As Arbie looked puzzled, I added, "We're after the stamps, remember? Edgar Berney is our best lead yet."

"Better than Stavoris?" she cried. "Better than Betterton?" Arbie sat in the taxi. "I don't believe this!"

"Oh, I'm still after the big fish, but it's the small fry who put us on the right trail."

"You're wasting your time with Berney," Arbie said. "Instead of getting the big fish, you'll be fishing up deadwood."

SEVEN

I called by the Science Division during coffee break next morning. Edgar Berney was shelving periodicals. He watched dead-pan as I approached. His brown eyes looked disdainfully at me over his hooked nose.

"You didn't get much sleep last night," I said.

Berney shrugged. "I...I...I slept okay."

"Well, you interrupted my sleep," I said sharply.

Berney looked at me uncomprehendingly.

"I can have you put away in a very ugly place, Edgar," I said. "You won't make a salary there, and you won't be able to support your father."

Berney looked glum.

"I'll cut this beating around the bush. I want to cooperate and maybe I can save your hide." I gave him a questioning look.

"O...Okay, Mr. Mack," Berney said. He looked as if he were consenting to be led away.

"Let's go down to the second floor stack," I suggested.

25

I led Berney down the stack stairwell, along by the windows to one where a rope was tied to a cross bar. I leaned out and pulled the rope up. "Here, undo this," I told Berney. "Where'd you get it?"

"C...C...Carpenter's Shop," Berney said, quickly loosening the knot and rolling up the rope.

"Did you get the wire from there too?"

Berney nodded reluctantly and stood waiting with a stoic expression.

"Why did you steal it?" I demanded.

Berney shrugged and smiled slightly. "Guess I just wanted it for myself."

"Where are the other ten volumes?"

"I'm bringing them back," Berney said.

"How long will it take you to get them?"

"C...C...Couple of h...hours."

I became suddenly very angry with Berney but controlled myself and said shortly, "Take annual leave until you bring them into my office. I'll be waiting for you. Now move!"

I watched Berney's thin body stride down the stack corridor and disappear behind a range of books. Picking up the rope Berney left behind, I dashed along the first stack, through the Jewish Division to the 42nd Street entrance and left the rope with the cloakroom attendant. Keeping out of sight, I had to wait only half a minute before Berney strode past and out the door onto 42nd Street. As I followed him, I recalled the years I had spent trailing staff members with library property to their homes. I knew that this was my most important trail job yet.

Berney went eastward along 42nd Street and stepped into a telephone booth. I waited five minutes until Berney stepped back into the street and headed south on Fifth Avenue. Block after block I trailed Berney through crowds of shoppers and tourists. At 31st Street, Berney turned east and eventually stepped into a doorway near Lexington Avenue. Rickety stairs led to a stamp collector's shop behind high, dirty windows of the corner room on the second floor over a delicatessen. I crossed over to read the nameplate on the door. "Winslow Margin. Stamp Dealer." My heart skipped a beat. Could Winslow be related to Homer Margin, the Chief Librarian?

I found a convenient doorway from where I could watch the dirty windows and the street door for Berney's reappearance. I turned over in my mind every conversation I had had with Homer for signs that revealed Homer was playing a game with me. I could find none. A long thirty minutes later Berney appeared at the street door. Folding an envelope double and stuffing it in his pocket, he strode up Lexington Avenue to 42nd Street and turned into Grand Central Station. I almost lost sight of him in the crowd, but, at the last second, I saw him on the stairway to the lower level. I wasn't sure, but I thought Berney glanced back at me to see if he was being followed. I dashed across the great hall, side-stepping travelers as I went, and sped down the stairs out into the lower level. There were just a few people hurrying to and from trains. I saw Edgar Berney by an open luggage locker along one wall pulling shopping bags out of the locker onto the floor. Berney looked round at me as if he had known I was behind him all the time.

"Yo...yo...yo...You can help me carry these," Berney smiled wickedly.

Grimacing, I picked up two bags with encyclopedia volumes in them and, together with Berney, who also carried two bags, headed without a word back to the Library.

I set the bags on the table in my office where I had put the two volumes earlier, checked through to see that the set was complete and then signaled Berney to shut the door and sit down. I wanted to shake the smugness out of him.

"You told me you took the whole encyclopedia for yourself," I said.

"Yeah, I did," Berney said. "I was gonna keep it in the locker, u...u...u... until the coast was clear."

Reluctantly, Berney took a package out of his pocket and handed it over. I found some of the George VI Coronation issue and several United Nations special issues. I handed the package back.

"Does it take you a half-hour to buy a simple lot like that?"

"I...I...I...I have to take care," Berney said with an undertone of resentment.

"You better take care," I warned him. "If I report you as a thief, the Library will fire you."

"Maybe," Berney said.

His confidence surprised me. Was he bluffing?

"I'll make a deal with you," I said. "I'll give you a week to prove to me that you're serious in helping me find the stamps stolen from the Library. If you can't show me cooperation, I'll report you to Mr. Bugofsky."

"O...O...Okay," Berney smiled wanly. "Th...Thanks, Mr. Mack."

I watched him go apprehensively. Berney was a picture of uncooperativeness. I phoned Homer Margin and asked him to bring a couple of pages to collect the encyclopedia volumes. Homer was jubilant. "Misshelved! That's incredible!"

"Say," I asked casually, "do you know who runs a store for stamp collecting on Lex and 31st?"

There was a long pause before Homer said quietly, "My brother runs it. But I can't tell you anything about it. I haven't spoken to him for ten years. Is it to do with the theft?"

"Don't worry," I said reassuringly. "I'm just checking."

Homer did not come with the pages to get the encyclopedia. Rather they appeared pushing a book truck on which they loaded the volumes sullenly as if they were members of a penal colony. I thought that it was unlike Homer not to want to be the first to see the return of his prize reference books. Perhaps the question about his brother had upset him.

My telephone rang. Bugofsky's raucous voice screamed in the higher registers about the encyclopedia.

"They've been returned," I said calmly. "A memo's on its way to you."

"Then what are you loafing in your office for?" Bugofsky demanded. "God, we'll be losing half the books in the Library if you don't get out and do your job." He hung up.

I did not intend to write a memo to Bugofsky or to anyone about the encyclopedia just yet because I could not mention Edgar Berney without risking Berney's termination. I called Arbuthnott Vine, but her voice on the answering recorder said she was "in the field" and to leave a message. I left none and went into the hallway and saw Bugofsky, stoned, moving mechanically toward the 40th Street exit to his club down the block. Bugofsky was early; it was only 2.15 p.m. Celebrating the return of the encyclopedia? I checked myself. I could not afford to be cynical toward my superiors; it might show. I channeled my cynical thoughts onto the reading public. This was the way public servants remained sane and survived in their jobs; sometimes they were justified.

A reader who habituated the Oriental Division approached me in the hallway. He was short and swarthy with a wild glint in his eye. He strutted as if leading a marching band in bedroom slippers. He clasped his tie tightly between his teeth. I moved aside lest the man suddenly break into a twenty-yard dash and knock me over. He was classified as a harmless scholar.

Arriving at the 42nd Street cloakroom, I picked up the rope I had left there, descended the stairs at the back of the cloakroom to the cellar and went to the Carpenter's Shop. The rope had been freshly cut off a reel. Near-by was a reel of wire from which Berney had cut a strand for his other exploit out the back window. There was a couple of carpenters about who took no notice of me. It would have been easy for Berney or anyone to help himself to equipment. I wondered why the carpenters needed reels of both rope and wire and asked what they used them for.

"Damned if I know," one of the men said dropping a screwdriver into the pocket of his smock. "We've only had them a couple of months."

I asked who ordered them. The carpenter took me into a cubicle and leafed through papers stuck on a filing needle. "I thought we still had the work order," he said. "Let's see. Ah, here it is. Mr. Betterton ordered them."

I went away feeling rather unhappy. Every time the trail led me to a Trustee I felt more alone. I went back to my office, locked my door, and tried to think. Images of Arbuthnott flashed here and there throughout my thoughts so that I found I could pull no pattern together. I called her again. This time she answered.

"Back from the field?"

"Rudy!" she cried excitedly. "I'm going to surprise you, baby!"

"Don't," I said. "I can't take it."

"I've found the Postmaster Provisionals," she announced.

"You have them?" I slid to the edge of my chair.

"I know where to get them," she said quietly. "Sharkey told me. A dealer named Winslow Margin contacted the Library. He's acting as middleman for a guy who'll sell them back to the Library for $200,000."

"How did you find out?" I asked disbelievingly.

"Sharkey asked me to meet him in a bar. He wants to up the ante on the Welfare Plan, you know, stuff like higher dentist insurance so management can get the benefits as well as the staff. I said I'd do it, if he'll give me info on the stamp theft."

"Was he drunk?" I asked.

"Of course he was drunk," she said impatiently.

"Well, how does he know?"

"I asked him that," she lowered her voice. "One of the secretaries in Stavoris's office makes photocopies of important stuff for him."

"I believe you," I said. "Did Stavoris contact the police?"

"No!" Arbie cried. "That's just it! They're afraid that if the police come in, they'll fuck up the whole deal."

"Who is they?" I asked impatiently.

"The Chairman of the Board and the Director. Who else!"

"Not Betterton?"

"No, they're keeping it to themselves. Look, darling, I gotta run to a grievance hearing at a branch in upper Manhattan. Let's meet for dinner at seven, and we'll talk."

"My place," I said. "I'll cook us an Indian curry."

"I'm all in favor of anything that gets you hot," she laughed. "So long, Rudy."

I was also was in favor of anything that got me hot. At the moment that "anything" was Arbuthnott Vine. Her news, though, was disconcerting. I could not imagine why Stavoris did not inform the police of this blackmail attempt. I wondered in what form the information had been recorded. Certainly not as a letter from the stamp dealer who most likely telephoned Stavoris to propose the deal. President Stavoris had a penchant for writing everything down meticulously. He wrote minutes to himself. It must have been a copy of one of his minutes that Bugofsky had obtained unscrupulously. Actually, it was Bugofsky's unscrupulousness that kept him in his job as the library business manager. Bugofsky had stored away a lot of interesting information on the Trustees and other members of the "management team."

It was late afternoon already. I would need an early start to prepare the curry for Arbie, and since Winslow Margin's stamp shop was on my way home, I felt justified in leaving work early.

When I reached the door of the stamp shop, I found that I had been walking faster than usual, perhaps out of excitement. I waited a moment to catch my breath before proceeding up rickety stairs. I pushed open a paint-flecked old wooden door to step into the stamp collector's haven. It was one large room walled with dirty glazed windows on two sides. There were three display cases full of stamps. At the far end of the room by the windows was an expansive table on which lay magnifying glasses, tweezers, small wooden stands and other paraphernalia associated with the world of the stamp collector. Bending over the table and inspecting a stamp through an eye glass under a strong lamplight was the dealer, alone. I saw at once the resemblance to Homer Margin: same height, same intense look, save that Winslow did not wear glasses, same round face, save that Winslow had a small mustache.

"Yes, what do you want?" His speech was more clipped but with the same inquisitorial undertone.

"Looking for some stamps," I said dryly. Winslow gave a visitor the feeling of trespassing.

"Any specialty?"

"Old masters," I said stopping to inspect the stamps in a display case.

Winslow looked disconcerted. "Old masters?"

"Stamps with paintings by the Old Masters," I said.

29

"I don't categorize them in that way," Winslow said sharply. "You won't find them packaged like that anywhere."

"True, very true," I said. "I hunt them down."

"You're welcome to look," Winslow said going back to work.

"Ah!" I said. "Here's the Laughing Cavalier by Franz Hals. I have that." Winslow made no comment.

"I like the Dutch masters," I continued. "Also, I like heroic scenes. The great romantic pictures by the French artists--like Gericault-- battle scenes-- Wolfe dying on the Plains of Abraham. Do you have stamps like that?" Winslow was absorbed in his study.

I eyed the large black safe a few yards from where Winslow stood. "I'm willing to pay well for your help."

Winslow stared sharply at me as if he thought me an eccentric. "What price range?"

"Well, hell, I've been collecting for years so I got all the common stamps," I said. "I'm willing to pay for the rare ones."

"As much as $15,000?" Winslow raised an eyebrow.

"Maybe," I said stepping forward. "If it's got a real dramatic scene-- something heroic."

"Is the landing of Columbus in America dramatic enough for you?" Winslow asked with slight impatience.

My heart did a little skip. "Who did the design?"

"It's a reproduction of the painting by Vanderlyn," Winslow explained testily. "It hangs in the Capitol Building in Washington, as you know," he added with a hint of sarcasm.

"Say, I'd like to see that!" I opened my eyes wide with enthusiasm.

Winslow held out a magnifying glass to me. "It's here. I've just been inspecting it," Winslow said.

I came round to Winslow's side of the table, took the glass and studied the stamp laid on a white sheet of paper. It was a 15-cent 1869 inverted center like those missing from the Library. The ornamental scroll work at the top and bottom was light brown. The second color, the Prussian blue reproducing the picture of the center, had been printed upside down. It was beautifully designed and engraved. I noted the ink of a postage mark.

"It's used," I said, disappointed. "Got any unused?"

"Might have," Winslow looked openly scornful. "But it costs five times as much."

I reared back. "My gosh! It should be cheaper, you know. The center's upside down."

"Precisely," Winslow said, sensing that he was not making a sale and taking back the magnifying glass.

"Do you have any right side up?" I asked.

Winslow shook his head angrily. "I'm closing up now," he said. Walking to the door he held it open.

"I'll be back, " I said smiling broadly. "Thanks for your time."

So, I thought when back on the street, Margin not only has the Postmaster Provisionals but also the 1869 Inverted Centers and possibly the 1909 starred perforateds. He could be arrested and his premises searched, but that would not solve the mystery of the theft and would not bring back the Inverted Jenny. If I informed Detective Buckle, I might screw up whatever President Stavoris was negotiating. Better to leave the whole matter to Stavoris for the time being.

At seven I was still cooking the curry. At seven-thirty the curry was ready, but Arbuthonott had not arrived. My phone rang. I assumed Arbie was canceling our date. I recognized the hoarse voice of Berney senior.

"My son's hurt bad," Berney reported sadly. "He wants to see you right away-- in Harlem Hospital."

"What happened?"

"He was beat up. He could've been killed if some boys didn't save him."

I penned a note to Arbie that I was leaving a key with the doorman and to help herself to the curry. I left it with the doorman and hailed a cab. As I drove to 135th Street, I penciled my expenses into my notebook. It was a long expensive taxi ride like this that reminded me that I couldn't afford such costs out of my salary.

Edgar Berney, senior, was waiting for me inside the visitor's entrance. His goatee looked whiter in the neon light. He beckoned me to follow onto a side elevator, took me to the fourth floor, and down the hallway to Edgar's room.

"He's put off taking sedatives so he can talk to you," Berney senior said and left me at Edgar's bedside.

His head bandaged, his face badly bruised, one arm in a sling, Edgar Berney opened his eyes to stare at me.

"Encyclopedia," Berney said softly. "Stole it for someone else."

I nodded sympathetically. "I know. A redhead named Macdonald who works for Continental Insurance."

Berney's eyes opened wider with surprise.

"Did he do this to you?" I asked.

"Maybe," Berney smiled wanly. "Got the books back from him this morning." He paused as if feeling sudden pain. "Told him I'd tell everything if he didn't give 'em back."

"Where do I find him?"

"T...T...Ten Bank Street, a...a...apartment 5A," Berney whispered. "A...A... Assumed name. He wa...wants the last t...t...two volumes."

"Okay, get some rest, Edgar." I waved out to a passing nurse. "Want those sedatives now?"

"Yeah," Berney grimaced. "Wa...Wa...Wanted to tell before I died."

"You're not going to die," I said. "Hang in there."

I looked for a public telephone in the hallway and called my number. Arbie was there. I told her the news.

"I'm going after the redhead," I said.

"Not without me!" she said.

"Don't be stupid, someone has to stay back in case something happens."

"Stupid! Christ Almighty! Rudy! You can't go into a den of killers alone!" She added four letter words while I turned the receiver away. "Besides," she cried, "you don't have your gun, do you?"

"No, I don't," I admitted.

"Well, it's here. I'll bring it to you."

"Okay, sweetheart."

"Meet me at McSorley's as soon as you can get there."

I smiled to myself as I hung up. She picked McSorley's Saloon only because women had not been allowed in it until women's lib knocked on its door. I was pleased with one thing. By guessing right that Macdonald was Berney's contact, I made points with Berney. I waved good-bye to Berney senior who was watchfully hanging around outside his son's room.

EIGHT

I found Arbie nursing a small beer in a booth at McSorley's. She handed me my gun and shoulder holster as soon as I sat down.

"What makes you think I'll have to use this?" I smiled strapping it on.

"This is the big time. You're not chasing absent-minded professors who wander out the front door of the Library with reference books under their arms."

"You want to see some action, don't you," I said. "We'll go to the apartment together, but you leave the talking to me. I'll play it by ear."

"But what are we after, Rudy?" She looked puzzled.

"First," I held up my index finger, "we want to know the connection between the theft of the encyclopedia and the theft of the stamps. Second, who Macdonald is working for."

"Aside from Continental Insurance and our dear President Stavoris," Arbie said.

"You're a bad influence," I said. "Before long you'll have me accusing the Mayor of New York."

"I wouldn't be surprised," Arbie said with a wicked smile. "He's an ex-officio member of the Library Board isn't he?"

"Come on!" I gave her a pull by the arm out of the booth.

Bank Street was badly lit. The building we wanted looked to be from the early part of the century, at which time it must have received its last coat of paint. The apartments and their occupants were listed in the vestibule. Opposite 5A we read "Storey." I pushed the buzzer and a male voice replied.

"I'm selling *Baker's Encyclopedia*," I said. "Are you interested?"

There was a long pause. "I'm interested." The voice was deep with a rough edge like that of the redheaded stamp aficionado. The door buzzer sounded, and I pushed open the door.

It was a walk-up.

"God-damn it!" Arbie cried. "Five flights! We'll be too exhausted to resist."

"You can stay here and wait for me," I said.

"Oh no! You have the gun. I need protection." Arbie began climbing behind me.

On the fifth floor, an apartment door stood open from which a shaft of light reflected on the dimly-lit corridor. A man stepped into the light as we approached. I recognized the slim redhead with the blue eyes and florid face who had gregariously spoken to me about the Library stamps. Luckily, he did not recognize me. He was also the redhead whose photograph I took with Buckle and who went by the name of Macdonald.

"Who are you?" the redhead demanded suspiciously.

"Friends of Edgar Berney," I said.

Puzzled the redhead stepped back. "Come in."

We stepped through a short hallway into a plushly-furnished room. I noted the sophisticated recording equipment and racks of records and tapes.

"Edgar was mugged," I explained.

"Sorry, sorry, very sorry," the redhead shook his head. "This is a dangerous city. I don't go out much at night. My name's Storey, by the way. Edgar asked you to see me? Sit down, please, sit down." He gestured Arbuthnott to an armchair with a dazzling smile.

I sank into a chair; it felt too comfortable for the situation I was in. "Edgar can't deliver the encyclopedia you wanted, but he has it and he knows you want it soon."

"Oh yes, yes, yes," said Storey. "Edgar is very good at finding items in secondhand book stores. Yes, I would like it as soon as possible."

"Well," I said slowly. "He's authorized us to deliver it. Just tell us when and where?"

"The buyer is in Buffalo, New York," Storey smiled. "I'm simply an agent. If you can give all the twelve volumes to me, I'll see that they are delivered quickly. What is your name, by the way?"

"I'm Rudy and this is Arbie Vine," I gestured to Arbie as if she were my wife.

"Vine!" Storey looked interested. "Any relation to the great Ellsworth Vine?"

"Wish I were," I said. "Could have learned a good tennis serve. But he spelled it 'Vines!'."

Storey laughed appreciatively. He looked directly at Arbie. "How did you meet Edgar Berney?"

"We've worked with him on many deals," Arbie said off-handedly. "He's reliable and so are his contacts usually." She looked sharply at Storey.

"You can trust me," Storey smiled broadly. "But he had me fooled. I thought he was an amateur."

"Speaking of being professional," Arbie said, "let's return to business. Can you pay us now?"

Storey's smile faded. "What do you want?"

"Sixty thousand," Arbie said.

"They are rare," I chipped in when Storey gazed at us in astonishment.

"Wait, wait, wait a minute here!" Storey put out a cautionary hand. "Did Edgar suggest that amount?"

"No," I said quickly. "We're handling the sale now."

"Edgar didn't give me a hint that it would be that much. This is a shock! I'll have to confer with my client in Buffalo and get back to you." Storey's eyes took on a hard glint.

"We'll get back to you," I said standing up.

33

"Don't be unreasonable," Storey warned, a hard edge creeping into his voice. "Where can I reach you?"

I held up one hand and escorted Arbie to the door with the other. "We'll be in touch tomorrow. You're in the book?"

"That's right," the redhead said angrily.

Arbie yanked the door open, and we hurried down the steps in silence as Storey stared after us.

In the street I said, "Sixty thousand!"

"Well, he's thinking it over," Arbie laughed. "That shows how valuable they are to him."

"They couldn't be worth more than three thousand." I shook my head in astonishment. "But one thing we found out is that they're intended for James New in Buffalo."

"Do you think Storey suspects us?" Arbie asked as we hailed a cab.

"He suspects us of holding him up," I said holding the cab door open for Arbie. "And I think he's uglier than he looks."

"Oh, I think he's ugly, ugly," Arbie said snuggling up to me in the back seat. "That's why I need a big strong detective tonight."

"Something tells me you'll get your wish," I said.

Arbie was singing before breakfast. I noticed that her voice was softer and the expletives had vanished from her speech. Our lovemaking had transformed her.

"I'm going to Washington for a rally, darling," she said over coffee. "Will you miss me?"

"How long?"

"Be back in two days, not long," she said dreamily.

I was secretly glad. I would be left alone to deal with Storey-cum-Macdonald. When I arrived at my office, my secretary told me to see Betterton right away.

Henry Betterton still looked out of place in the small office which was actually an ante-room to President Stavoris's richly ornamented office. His large footballer's frame seemed to dwarf everything around him. He looked very serious.

"Sit down, Rudyard. Do you remember that I told you an Inverted Jenny had turned up in James New's collection--poor James!"

"You know him?" I feigned surprise.

"I knew him." Betterton handed me a Buffalo newspaper dated the previous day. A column on the front page announced his death. The subheading questioned suicide or homicide. "We had some dealings in a business way. A nice old fellow."

"How did he get the Inverted Jenny?" I asked innocently.

"The police do not know. It's unlikely we shall discover the mystery now." Betterton took back the newspaper and tossed it in a looping pass into a vertical file drawer open behind him. "His death, at least, gives us the opportunity of approaching the lawyers of his estate on the matter. As you know, we were not absolutely sure that the stamp he had was stolen from us."

"Are we sure now?" I asked.

"We are going to make sure," Betterton said with annoyance. "That is why I am talking to you now. I want you to determine if the stamp in his estate is our Inverted Jenny."

"Excuse me for interrupting," I smiled, "but is that not the job of the Manhattan Burglary Squad?"

"It is," Betterton said patiently. "They can't determine if it is or if it isn't. We have to know before the estate is broken up if we want that stamp returned to our collection. Now, I'm entrusting this important work to you, and I have written this "To Whom It May Concern" letter for you to that purpose." He handed me an unsealed envelope in which there was a letter. "It designates you as the Library's representative in this matter. You show it to the lawyers of the estate."

"You want me to go to Buffalo?" I asked with surprise. I had never before been sent beyond the outskirts of the City.

"That's where the lawyers live," Betterton intoned. I could almost read the exasperation in his eyes.

I thought I would test him on what he knew of Winslow Margin's ransom demand for the Postmaster Provisionals. "Do you know if James New had the rest of the stamps?" I asked casually. "Such as the Postmaster Provisionals."

"They haven't surfaced yet," Betterton grimaced. "But sooner or later they will."

So Stavoris, as President and Chairman of the Board, was keeping the ransom demand to himself. "You don't think," I asked slowly, "that James New's death is connected with the Inverted Jenny?"

"How should I know?" Betterton looked amused. "I hope it is not. But that's your job. Good luck, Rudyard. Call me if you need anything."

I felt the pressure as I walked along the marble hallway. Library management had a subtle way of casually asking you to do something yet somehow implying that your job performance would be measured by the results you obtained. The more impossible the request, the more casual the tone, the more threatening the penalty for failure. I was exempt from Arbie's trade union. I had no defense against arbitrary dismissal, which was why, maybe, Arbuthnott saw me as a slave to management's viewpoint.

I had to endure the slave's treatment once again, I thought as I stepped into Bugofsky's office. The blond, shapely secretary asked me to wait a moment. It was just a moment before the gangling Amos Anders strode awkwardly out of Bugofsky's room. He gave me a perfunctory nod as he passed. I stepped in to find Bugofsky smiling broadly, his teeth glinting from the side of his mouth, his black hair greased back, and his brown eyes sharp with satiric humor.

"Well, Rudyard, you didn't collide with the Big Joke?"

I assumed he meant Anders and smiled genially as I sought a chair. It was fairly early in the morning, and Bugofsky appeared to be in a genial mood.

"What have you been up to in the halls of this glorious institution?" Bugofsky continued. "You're not on the job here enough, Rudyard." His tone became menacing. "Don't screw around with this stamp farce. I want you policing this place. Do you understand? I want you walking the halls with your walkie-talkie." His voice rose angrily. "I want you to oversee those bastards; I want you to stop them from lifting this place right from under our arses." He paused and smiled at his use of the word. "It'd serve them right, though, wouldn't it?"

By "them" I assumed he meant Anders and the rest of the front office.

"It's about *Baker's Encyclopedia*," I began.

"You got that back on the shelves yet?" Bugofsky glowered.

"It's back, but I want to take it out again." I explained briefly my contact with Storey. "He may even pay as much as sixty thousand."

The mention of money unsettled Bugofsky. He suddenly became reasonable, more human. He was willing to permit me to use the volumes as I saw fit; he did not want to hear the details. "But keep quiet about the money," he said. "Don't tell a soul, except me. Keep me informed." He waved for me to quit his office.

I found Homer Margin in the main reading room writing out a service review on one of the librarians. From the look of the boxes checked, I figured that that particular librarian would never be promoted. A momentary malice of supervisors can ruin careers in the Library. The staff members had no defense. No other supervisor enjoyed his god-like power so thoroughly as Homer. Joy sang in Homer's eyes when he made out service reviews: life to him, death to her, reprieve for him.

"Yes," Homer said, looking up and covering the service review with his arm. "What can I do for you, Mr. Mack?"

"I'm taking the encyclopedias," I said, "if you don't mind."

"I do mind," Homer retorted sharply. "We need them on the shelves."

"It won't be for long," I said. "Mr. Bugofsky's orders."

Homer jumped up in agitation. "I wish the Business Office would stop sticking its nose in librarians' business." He put the service review into a drawer. "But if you must have them, you must." He led the way into the reading room and beckoned to a page to fetch a truck. The twelve volumes sat in their accustomed place on the shelves. "You are going to have to sign out for them," Homer said severely. He pulled a request slip from his pocket, filled in the main entry and the number of volumes, and gave it me. "You are responsible for it."

"I have an important question," I said signing the slip and writing my address as the Business Office. "Reference books on the open shelves like this encyclopedia are never allowed out of this room, right?"

"Right," Homer said, "unless we give a reader permission to take a volume or two to the photocopy room. And we keep records of that."

"Never for any other reason?" I emphasized.

"Never." Homer looked very nervous. "If I caught one of my librarians allowing a reference book out of these reading rooms for any other reason, I would suspend him." Homer looked like a little tiger bristling behind his glasses.

"Let me put it like this," I said, as Homer directed a page to put the volumes on the truck. "Within the last month, aside from the period of the theft, have these volumes ever left this room?"

"Well," Homer said, "we can check the xeroxed records."

"Aside from that," I smiled, recognizing the perverse streak in Homer. "I mean for reasons that were unofficial, at any time."

Homer looked uneasy. "Once only," he admitted. "On my authority."

I waited patiently.

"Where do you want these taken?" Homer asked.

I directed the page to leave all twelve volumes in my office.

"On your authority?" I asked.

"I gave special permission for a very important writer to remove the volumes to the Allen Room for two or three days."

I thought of the biographer I met on the day of the stamp theft who had forgotten his key to the Allen Room, which by the way was located off the first floor lobby, near the Miller Stamp Collection.

"Do you have the request slip?" I asked.

Homer blushed. "It wasn't necessary. I saw to it that the volumes were returned on time."

I smiled. Homer liked to please the great, that is, very important writers. "And when was that? On the morning before the stamp theft?" I suggested.

"I believe it was," Homer nodded, looking more embarrassed.

"I see." I left Homer standing there, wondering.

I was somewhat more certain of how the theft was conducted, but I was no closer to the reason for it or to the mastermind behind it.

When I reached my office, the page was just wheeling the encyclopedia volumes into it. I carefully inspected each volume. The linings inside the back covers of the volumes had been slit open to make small pockets in which I found nothing, except for the last two volumes. Tucked into the linings of them were stamps--from the Miller Collection! So this was the connection between the thefts of the stamps and of the encyclopedia. Berney smuggled the stamps out of the Library when he carried out the volumes of the encyclopedia. Storey must have known what the volumes contained.

I dialed Storey's telephone number and wondered, now that James New was dead, whether Storey would still be interested in the volumes. I suspected that he would be, especially in the last two.

Storey answered. "When can you make delivery?" he asked.

"For sixty thousand," I insisted.

"You're bloodsuckers," Storey said and cursed, "but when you get the goods, I'll pay."

"Tomorrow at noon on the Central Park side of Columbus Circle. Come alone," I warned.

Storey laughed. "Bring your wife. She's cute."

"She's marching for peace," I said. "I'll be alone."

"Central Park is kind of public," Storey said. "Aren't you afraid of counting that much money in the open?"

"That's a drug corner," I said. "It's insignificant. We'll look like paupers."

Storey laughed and hung up.

I sat at my desk and practiced pulling my revolver from my shoulder holster. I never had to pull it out before. So far Library patrons had not required such extreme treatment. I decided to visit a firing range for an hour or two in the afternoon.

NINE

As I was getting ready to leave at three in the afternoon, after Bugofsky toddled off to his club, I received a message over my walkie-talkie to go right away to the President's Office.

William Stavoris and Amos Anders were waiting. Their expressions were grim. My heart sank. I expected to hear that I was being replaced by an experienced private detective. I could even hear Stavoris say in studied sympathy, "Too bad, after your years of good service, but that's life, Mr. Mack."

"Making progress on the stamp case, Mr. Mack?" Anders asked pleasantly. His long angular face gave no hint of displeasure.

"I believe I am, sir." I sat in the chair which Anders pointed to and felt uneasy. "I hope my work is satisfactory."

"Yes, yes," Anders nodded appreciatively. "We think it is a very important job you are doing. We'll be depending on you a good deal from now on."

I looked at him in amazement.

"We have decided to bring you into our confidence," Stavoris announced, shifting his rotund yet muscled body aggressively forward in his chair. He had the easy conspiratorial air of an executive with years of boardroom experience. It was as if he were offering me the key to the executive washroom. "It is a delicate matter and we consider that you are the man to trust with handling it. It is absolutely imperative, let me emphasize, that what we discuss here today go no farther than the three of us. We have not informed the police as yet because we are afraid that by doing so we might jeopardize this delicate situation."

"We have not...ah...spoken to Messrs. Betterton and Bugofsky," Anders said. "We will do so after we do our own investigation. We think that if we use the greatest discretion, we can negotiate the return of at least some of the stamps."

"Which is where you come in," Stavoris said, taking over the conversation. He gave a quick glance at Anders and continued. "We have been informed that a stamp dealer, acting for a client, is willing to sell us back the Postmaster Provisional stamps stolen from the Library. He does not know his client's identity. He simply talks to him over the telephone."

"I think I know the stamp dealer you are referring to," I nodded. "He's the brother of the Chief of the General Research Division, isn't he?"

Stavoris's mouth dropped. He turned to Anders. "Is his last name 'Margin'?"

Anders confirmed it nervously. "The Chief of the General Research Division is Homer Margin. I didn't know there was a connection."

I was glad to have made the point. It upset their attitude of condescension.

"The same dealer may have the Inverted Centers which were stolen from the Miller Collection," I said casually. "He tried to sell me one."

"He did?" Stavoris's eyes opened wide in utter astonishment; then they flashed and took on a cunning look. "He could be hoodwinking us. He may have the Postmaster Provisionals himself."

"I don't think so," I said. "I think he is really fronting for someone."

"Good," Stavoris relaxed. He looked at Anders and then at me. I could see they were beginning to see me anew, with a little more respect. "I see we chose the right man for the job." He paused. "By the way, this Margin fellow says he can't help us if the police are involved."

"But if he himself has some of the stamps...." Anders said cautiously and half questioningly.

"He can easily say he has not got them," Stavoris said. "He can claim to have never seen them. No! We need Mr. Mack's talents to deal with Mr. Winslow Margin."

"Are you prepared to buy them back?" I asked.

Stavoris scratched his chin. "The thief can't sell them on the open market because they are easily recognizable. It is possible then to buy them back for less than the market price. But the Library is really too poor to pay anything. It was even too poor to afford the proper security for the stamps in the first place."

I recognized the poverty argument. It was recited whenever it was time to raise the staff's wages.

"Tell me," I said genially. "Have you collected stamps, Mr. Stavoris."

Stavoris did not blink. "I did when I was a boy, but I gave my collection to my nephew. Why do you ask?"

"No particular reason," I smiled and stood up. "I was wondering what the motive behind the stamp theft could be."

"Greed, Mr. Mack," Anders said and laughed abruptly. "Just simple greed."

Stavoris stood up and, giving the impression of great strength contained in a short, rotund body, walked with me to the door which he opened. "Be discreet and keep in touch with me on every step you take."

I was beginning to feel like a split personality. Each faction in the Library management had put its full confidence in me--confidentially. It was possible each was using me against the other. And somewhere in all this mess was the mastermind who was profiting from the theft. Then again, just how was he profiting? Was it simply greed as the Director had said? Or was there something more subtle, like an obsessed collector's satisfaction involved? If I could determine a motive, I might dissipate some of the turmoil of confusion that seemed to swirl around in my mind when I considered all the possibilities.

At the firing range, I had been practicing for less than an hour when I noticed Detective Buckle of the Manhattan Burglary Squad watching me. Since the police had their own practice ranges, Buckle was obviously just checking out the range's clientele. Buckle saw that I had caught him watching, and he came over to me.

"Not a bad shot," Buckle said in the most agreeable voice he had ever used with me. "Library expecting another robbery?"

"Be prepared, that's our motto," I said and took aim at the target.

Buckle waited until I shot. "If word gets around that the Library's guards are good with weapons, the crooks will shoot first," he warned. "Better that you guys not carry guns."

"Just two or three of the Library security have them," I explained. "Just precautionary."

Buckle shrugged. "Don't say I didn't warn you."

"Say," I put my gun away. "Any new developments in the stamp theft?"

Buckle's fat face took on a guarded expression. "We're waiting for a sale," he said.

"That could take years," I said.

"Patience--that's what you learn when you become a detective." Buckle gave me a condescending look.

"What about the redhead?" I asked. "Has he surfaced?"

"Nope," Buckle looked straight at me. "Let us know if you see him again," he smiled and walked away.

I could not explain Buckle's evasiveness. Was Buckle in league with Storey? If he was, maybe he knew about the encyclopedia transaction that was scheduled to take place. That could lead to complications. I went straight home to cook dinner and retire early to bed with a brandy and a book about the Greek Isles. I waited for inspiration to show me the way.

At eleven-thirty the next morning, carrying two shopping bags of heavy books, I left the Library and took a taxi to Columbus Circle. I took up a position by the stone gateway to Central Park. I watched well-dressed whites approach small groups of Hispanics and blacks which broke up while one of their members exchanged something with the whites, and the groups reformed and joked and shuffled about. I watched the pigeons peck in the dirt and fly on and off the low stone wall. At twelve, I watched the traffic round the Circle. At five past the hour, a blue sedan came out of the traffic and stopped in the road leading into the park. Storey sprang out. There was a driver waiting in the car. It was hard to see, but he didn't look like Buckle.

"I told you to come alone," I said.

"Oh, I couldn't!" Storey threw out his hands in a gesture of hopelessness. "My partner doesn't trust me." He looked at the bags. "You got the right books?"

I handed them over. Storey pulled out a volume to check the title.

"Okay," he said, dropping the volume back in the bag. He pulled a fat envelope out of his pocket. "It's in thousand dollar bills. You gonna count it here?" he smiled.

I opened the envelope, looked in to see the denomination of one of the bills, and then slipped it into my coat pocket. "I trust you," I said.

Storey ran back to the car and set the bags on the car seat while he and his companion looked at the volumes. I watched until I saw Storey rear back and charge furiously out of the car up to me.

"You goddamn cheat!" he yelled. "There're only ten volumes!"

"I couldn't carry more," I said calmly.

"Gimme back the money," Storey grabbed at my pocket.

40

"Wait!" I pulled away. "I can bring you the other two volumes. Why all the excitement?"

Storey looked less agitated. "We gotta have a complete set. Ten volumes are just no good."

"All right." I walked to the car with him. "We'll make other arrangements." I pulled out the two bags, set them on the ground, and handed the envelope back. Storey looked in it suspiciously before he sat in the car.

I took note of Storey's companion. He was thin, swarthy complexioned, thin mustached, sad-expressioned and in his mid-thirties.

"Don't play games with me again," Storey warned. "I want the complete set."

I watched the car disappear into the traffic circle. I picked up the bags and took just a few steps when I was stopped by a police officer.

"What ya got there?" the cop demanded.

I showed him the contents of the bags. "For my library," I said.

"Oh yeah, stand straight and put your arms at your sides," the cop commanded.

A second policeman came up behind me. The first cop patted the pockets of my coat.

"He's got a gun," he told his companion.

"I'm with security," I said, feeling somewhat embarrassed that passers-by and some of the drug pushers were gathering round.

"Oh yeah," the cop said. "Show me."

I took out my wallet and gave the cop my Identification Card.

"He's okay," the cop said to his companion. "We gotta be careful," he told me. "There's a lot of funny business in this neighborhood."

I felt like pointing out the funny business, but I picked up the shopping bags and hailed a cab. I could not be sure that I had not been set up. If the cops had caught me with the money on a drug corner, there was no telling what sort of trouble I could have got into.

When I returned to the Library, I called up Homer Margin to send down a page with a book truck to take the encyclopedia back to the shelves. I had verified my suspicion that Storey believed that the remaining stamps were in the last two volumes, but, of course, I had removed them. At the same time I suspected that Storey may have found out about me. For the first time, I felt a personal danger. I called Allegheny Airlines and arranged to take a flight to Buffalo that afternoon. I worried whether one hour on the firing range had been long enough.

TEN

I hired a car when I checked into a hotel in downtown Buffalo. After New York, the long straight streets flanked by two and three storey buildings gave me a feeling of flatland. The avenues seemed endless and the public transport uncertain.

41

After dinner, I drove to the funeral home where James New lay in rest. Scanning the visitor's book, I recognized one name with alarm: "John Macdonald, Continental Insurance, N.Y.C." It was entered about an hour ago. Three men were talking quietly in one corner of the room. I guessed they were friends or business associates. Apart from these, only one other man was in the room. He was in his sixties and stood contemplating the floor near the coffin, which was closed. I sensed a professional air about him and guessed that he might be the man I was looking for. I introduced myself. I was right. The man gave his name as Marshall Harriman from the law firm looking after New's estate.

After I showed him Betterton's letter of introduction, Harriman said, "Henry Betterton knows we can do nothing until after the funeral." Harriman's heavy-set frame gave him an aspect of solid respectability.

"Which is tomorrow, isn't it?" I said.

"Tomorrow at four in the afternoon," Harriman confirmed. "It will be better if we talk outside." He led the way out of the funeral home. "We can talk in my car."

I followed him to the side driveway and got into the passenger side of a Lincoln Continental. Harriman sat in the driver's seat.

"The Library just wants to be sure the stamps are in a safe place," I said pleasantly.

"We have no responsibility in that matter until after the funeral," Harriman said. "Even then, we cannot guarantee anything. Mr. New had heard of the Library's concern about a particular stamp, but his position was that he purchased it through legitimate channels. We have to respect his wishes. We have assured Mr. Betterton that we will investigate its origins thoroughly."

"Where is the stamp now?" I asked.

"I assume it is in Mr. New's safe where he kept his valuables. He has quite a number of valuable stamps which are now the property of his heirs."

"Who are they?" I asked.

"Two sons and a daughter. His wife died seven years ago."

I paused as if to render homage to the tragedy of death. I sensed that Harriman regarded me as an intrusion on the family's grief. The lawyer's jowly face wore an expression of polite indifference, and his small brown eyes seemed to lie in wait for my next question.

"Will the circumstances of his death delay the settling of the estate?"

"I am afraid it will," Harriman said, stirring uncomfortably behind the driver's wheel. "You see, if it is determined that Mr. New committed suicide, the question of the soundness of his mind will have to be resolved. This is especially important because he made his last will just a week before his death."

"That must be worrisome for you," I said.

"It does give us concern," Harriman admitted. He looked in the rear-view mirror. "Ah, will you excuse me, please. Some of Mr. New's friends have arrived."

"I shall be in touch after the funeral," I said as we stepped out of the car. "Thank you for your indulgence."

"Not at all," he nodded politely.

42

I watched Harriman step quickly to catch the visitors before they reached the door of the funeral home. I drove to my hotel, went to bed, and watched television until I fell asleep.

In the morning, I drove to the stores of stamp dealers in Buffalo. Three dealers became evasive when I asked about James New; a fourth was more forthcoming. He was sprightly and talkative and gave me the impression that he liked to gossip about the rich who frequented his shop because it made his business more important. When I informed him that I was a detective, the dealer changed his manner. He now appeared ready to bring me into his confidence.

"Charming chap, Mr. New. Not your regular business type, if you know what I mean. Used to belong to the Philatelic Society here where I knew him quite well, you know. Even got to see his collection on occasion. Fabulous stamps, really fabulous! You know, he had items like the Canadian 5-cent Beaver."

"How long ago did you last see his collection?" I asked.

"Oh, two or three years now. He used to come in here regular, but not for a long time. I believe he bought his stamps through a sort of consortium of private collectors. So, in the last several years, he'd just come in here for the conversation. I couldn't compete with an international consortium as they're likely all millionaires!"

"Ever see the American 24-cent airmail inverted?"

"The Inverted Jenny!" The dealer smiled. "I heard that rumor. He was the sort of chap who'd get his hands on it. But he didn't buy it from me." He adopted an innocent look.

"Do you think he was murdered?" I asked suddenly.

The dealer seemed stunned for a moment, then recovered, thought for a moment and continued in his confidential manner. "I know he did not commit suicide. He was not the type. Besides, why would he? He was too old." He laughed, then nudged me half-jokingly and said, "Don't ask me who killed him. You should ask one of his multi-millionaire friends."

At two-thirty in the afternoon, I drove by the New residence in an exclusive residential section of the city. The large house sat far back from the road. A low stone fence fronted the property. I parked a block away and waited ten minutes when I saw the family mourners appear from the driveway in two black cars and drive by. I got out and walked down a side street until I reached the back of the New property. Quickly passing through the back gate, I crossed the lawn and concealed myself under the lilac bushes behind the back porch. I had not long to wait. A car pulled up at the back entrance. I recognized the thin, mustached face of the man who was driving it. Storey stepped out, his red hair looking rich and full. He walked through the gate, climbed onto the back porch and rang the bell.

The maid answered. She was a young woman and had barely opened the door when Storey pushed it with his knee wide open and stepped in. The door swung back but did not click shut. I saw the thin man in the car watching the back door like a hawk. I could not move. I could only hope to catch Storey somehow as he was leaving.

Then barely two minutes later, a police squad car cruised slowly down the street and pulled up beside Storey's car. The thin man had seen it coming and pretended to be scribbling notes on a pad. There was a brief conversation. The thin man drove off. The squad car stayed a moment while the policeman on the driver's side scanned the back part of the house. He seemed satisfied and drove away. I quickly left my hiding place, leaped onto the porch and pushed through the door. I closed it firmly and proceeded through the kitchen down a hallway toward the front of the house.

Presently I heard voices ahead on my right. I crept to an open door and looked through the crack. I saw Storey kneeling at a wall safe. By moving a bit, I saw the maid sitting on a straight-back chair facing Storey. She had been made to sit on her hands.

The maid was crying. "I'm telling you all his stamps were stolen. The police couldn't find any of them."

"Believe me, baby, I don't want to hurt you. But if you don't tell me how to open this thing, I'm going to have to."

"But there are no stamps in there!" she cried.

"I won't know that till I open it, will I?" Storey reasoned with her. "If they're gone, you've got nothing to lose."

"Oh!" she put her head down in exasperation. "All right. Mr. New kept the combination in the front of that big volume of Shakespeare's Plays on the shelf up there."

Storey seized the volume and, flipping over the front cover, took out a piece of paper and began tumbling the lock on the safe. In a moment, he opened the safe and brought out a handful of papers.

"Nothing here," he said, his deep voice rasping with disappointment, "just property deeds and that crap."

The maid stopped crying. "I told you," she pouted.

"Listen to me," Storey said sharply. "You see that wall clock? You watch that for ten minutes. Don't make a move before then. I might still be around here someplace."

The maid said nothing, but the relief on her face said more than words could express. I stepped into the room across the hall. I heard Storey walk down the hallway into the back of the house. I stepped back to look through the crack in the door. The maid sat stock still. The safe door gaped open. I glided quietly down the hall with my gun at the ready. When I came to the back door, I looked through the door window to see Storey standing in the street and looking impatiently up and down it. Then Storey waved angrily. His car drove up, picked him up, and drove away. I left the house and returned to my car.

If James New had ever had the Library's Inverted Jenny, it appeared to have vanished. There were several possible explanations: New was murdered and the murderer stole the stamps; New gave the stamps to someone, maybe his lawyers for safekeeping; New sold his stamps before he died; the stamps were somewhere else in New's house. One thing was sure: Storey did not know where they were.

I drove to the Episcopalian Burial Ground where the newspaper had reported James New was to be buried. The mourners were parking their cars and walking to the grave site. I joined them.

I was working on the theory that the murderer always returns to the scene of the crime, that there is a link between the victim and the criminal, that the

44

criminal act becomes a part of the psychology of the criminal, that it is deeply repressed into his subconscious and that it will impel the criminal to recapture the moment of intimacy with the victim which he had at the moment of the crime itself. In the case of James New, I reckoned that moment would be in the lowering of New's coffin into the grave.

A large crowd of people had come to the burial site. I slowly circled it as I looked at the mourning faces. I spotted plainclothes detectives, business associates, and a handful of New's relatives. Suddenly, I stopped as if rooted to the ground. Just beyond the relatives was the red head and sullen countenance of Storey whose gaze was fixed on me. As the final rites were spoken, we stared at each other between heads and shoulders and across the grave. I supposed that Storey, posing as John Macdonald of Continental Insurance, feared I would address him as Storey, and would have liked nothing better than to add my corpse to the one being lowered into the grave.

When the burial was concluded, I tried to make my way through the dispersing crowd to Storey but found that he had disappeared in a hurry.

"Mr. Mack!"

I looked round unable to determine where the call came from. My hand automatically went to my gun. I was afraid Storey might be calling me to a show-down.

"Mr. Mack!" The voice this time was commanding, not threatening.

To my astonishment, I saw Henry Betterton step out of a crowd of men with the lawyer, Harriman. They approached me between the gravestones. The thick-bodied Harriman looked like a linebacker running interference for the swift-footed Betterton.

"You look surprised to see me," Betterton smiled handsomely. "I had to come up this way on business, so I thought I'd see Mr. Harriman about our missing stamps. How have you been making out?"

"Running into closed doors," I said.

"Never mind," Betterton patted my shoulder. "Mr. Harriman gave me some interesting news. It seems that when he turned his will over to the firm last week, Mr. New included a memorandum which asked that, immediately after his death, his Inverted Jenny be donated to the New York Public Library. What do you think of that, Mack?"

"You understand," Harriman interrupted. "I could not inform you of this until this moment."

"It seems, however," Betterton continued, taking me by the shoulder, "that New's stamp collection has disappeared. His family haven't seen it, and it's not in his security boxes."

"It is important to point out," Harriman said gravely, "that his donating the stamp to the Library in no way suggests that he had the stamp which was stolen from the Library."

Betterton gave me a quick wink. "The Library would be the last to suppose that," he said.

"Of course we have alerted Interpol," Harriman said. "A collection of the rarity of Mr. New's would be highly detectable, I should think."

"If we find out who murdered Mr. New," I said, "we'll be on the trail of the missing stamps."

"So you, too, suspect it was not suicide? The police, also, suspect it was murder, but they have no clues," Harriman admitted. "Apparently, the bullets that killed Mr. New were not from the gun that was found in his hand."

We reached the roadside by now, and cars were starting up and moving by us.

"Do you want a lift back to New York?" Betterton asked. He seemed to want to know me better and to suggest that the long ride back would give him that opportunity.

"Sorry, I still have some business here," I said apologetically. I suspected that Betterton really wanted to save the Library the cost of my air fare.

"Suit yourself." Betterton opened his car door and waved a friendly good-bye.

I walked quickly to my car and drove at top speed to the shop of the dandified stamp dealer with whom I had spoken in the morning. The dealer broke off with a customer when he saw me and approached with a warm smile.

"Did they put old James away properly?" he asked.

"Yes," Mack said, "but they lost his stamp collection. Will you keep your eyes and ears open." I gave him my card. "What's your name?"

"Frank Aragon," the dealer said, studying the card. "Oh, I respect libraries. The pillars of civilization."

I looked sharply at him for any sign of sarcasm and, finding none, said, "We're sure New had our Inverted Jenny." I lowered my voice as I noticed the other customers watching us. "He could have been murdered for it."

"That's very, very true, Mr. Mack. I have had customers who would murder me for a stamp if I couldn't sell it to them." Aragon looked round cautiously. "That's the sort of passion that keeps me in business."

"Any idea who'd want it, Frank?" I asked.

"Yes, indeed," Aragon smiled. "I can recite a list of the leaders of organized crime in New York State; any one of them could have murdered old James New for that stamp."

"I know," I nodded. "It looks hopeless."

"It could be in a deposit box in a Swiss bank," Aragon said. "I don't mean to rub it in."

"Do you know Winslow Margin?" I asked abruptly.

Aragon looked startled. "Stamp dealer in New York? Yes."

"Is he a fence for stolen stamps?"

"Very much so. He's in the big time."

"He's offered to sell us back our Postmaster Provisionals. Can you find out who he's acting for?"

"I'll try," Aragon said. "I'm coming to New York next week. Maybe I can be of help."

"That's great of you, Frank," I said gratefully.

"Don't mention it. When anyone steals public property you can count on me to help catch the culprit. Worst crime in the world--stealing from the public." He gave me a quick little smile.

46

I headed for the airport in a buoyant mood sustained all the way to New York by the thought that Arbuthnott would be back from Washington.

ELEVEN

"Goddamn crumbs!" Arbuthnott shouted when I entered my apartment. "You should've been there, Rudy. We got whacked over the head and generally shoved around by the pigs. All because we don't want the fat cats to make any more money out of deadly weapons."

"Your reasoning sounds innocent enough," I said, dropping my suitcase into my bedroom and coming into the living room where Arbie lay sprawled over the couch. "But it's always the innocents who get hurt."

"And how!" Arbie felt her head. "I thought I was done for."

"Is the pain still there?" I took her head in my hands.

"It'll never go away," she smiled and, putting her arms about my neck, kissed me long and hard. I took hold of her breasts and she pushed my hands away. "Your dinner is ready, sir. It's been waiting two hours for you." She led the way into the small dining area. She had the table set for two with two candles burning in the center. The vegetables were being kept warm on the side table and the steak had just been broiled.

I smiled appreciatively. "You're quite a girl, rough-housing it in Washington and romancing it in New York."

"Wait till you taste it," she said, putting my plate before me and her plate on her table mat. She dashed into the kitchen and returned with a bottle of white wine which she handed me to open. "I'm just trying to give my life some balance, for sanity's sake."

I poured the wine.

"Okay, Rudy, now taste it."

I cut off a piece of steak. It seemed to melt in my mouth. I nodded. I took some mashed potato, followed it with spinach, and nodded again. I took a drink of wine.

"You can eat it," I said. "It's really quite good."

"Thank you," she said. "Does that mean I can come back another time?"

"That means you can stay," I smiled.

"Oh no, it doesn't!" she laughed. "My idea of paradise does not include cooking for a man."

I laughed with her, but I was a bit upset with myself for making the invitation. It had just slipped out and now remained between us as part of our relationship-- a sort of open door policy.

"Now tell me what I'm dying to hear," Arbie said.

"What's that?" I said warily.

"What's that!" Arbie threw up her arms. "What did you do in Buffalo? Is it too embarrassing to relate?"

Relieved, I told her about the theft of New's stamps.

"God!" she said. "I wouldn't have tracked Storey into that house for all the love in the world."

"So it all leaves me with unanswered questions," I sighed.

"And no corpus delecti," Arbie reminded me. "I suggest we go after Winslow, the stamp dealer. He's the only reasonable son-of-a-bitch we've got. I mean, all the others are screwed up just the way we are."

"Including the trustees?" I said mischievously.

"Including all but one of the trustees," Arbie said with emphasis. "You'll see I'm right."

"I've already met Winslow Margin," I said. "What else can I do?"

"Let's look in his store," Arbie suggested. "It's Friday night and it's ten o'clock; if he was gonna have any of New's stamps, he'd have them by now. They'd be in his store for a short time. Tomorrow, being Saturday, he'll get rid of them, at least, he won't have them after the weekend. So we gotta move our asses now, Rudy, old boy!"

"A break-in," I mused, realizing she was serious. "We'd better not get caught."

"Use your detective I D card," Arbie said.

"Oh yeah?" I said between mouthfuls. "I can see Buckle's face when he sees us behind bars."

"Never mind," Arbie said. "Think of his face when we come up with the Inverted Jenny."

Finishing the main course, we decided to leave immediately, though not without misgivings on my part.

"Dessert's gonna be a surprise," Arbie said.

"I hope we live to eat it," I grimaced. "I'm a cautious man. You bring out something in me that scares the hell out of me."

"You're not searching some kleptomaniac's apartment for pages razored out of *Scientific American* this time. This is the big time, Rudy."

By consulting the telephone book, we found that Winslow Margin lived on Lexington Avenue about two blocks from his store. It was near enough to walk. We passed by Margin's home address--apartments in a brownstone, looking seedy and rundown like the drunks that lay on the steps of the houses along the street.

When we came to the corner opposite to the stamp store perched in shabby decline above the darkened delicatessen, I asked Arbie to wait in the shadows. Pulling up my coat collar and setting my hat low over my forehead, I walked alongside the cars parked on the south side of 31st Street. About half-way up the block, I saw what I hoped I would not see: a thin, mustached man, smoking a cigarette at the wheel of a blue sedan. I hurried by, satisfied that he had not recognized me, and walked round the block back to Arbie.

"It was lucky you suggested we come," I said. "Storey's in there."

"Oh no! Oh God!" Arbie said.

"Don't worry," I said. "Better he makes the break-in than us. But we have to find another entrance. His friend is watching the front door."

We crossed the street, passed by the delicatessen and a funeral home, and slipped into the shadows of a vacant parking lot. A wire fence stood between us and the iron ladder of the fire escape leading to Winslow Margin's store.

"I'm too old for this," I said, climbing over the fence and taking care not to catch my clothes on the ends of the wires. "You stay here and give me two whistles if there's trouble." At times like this, I wanted to be tall like Betterton.

Arbie looked round to see if we were being observed. Passers-by in the street could not see into the darkened lot. I scaled the wall by the drain-pipe until I could reach over to grab the bottom rung of the ladder. I worked my hands to the second, third, and fourth rungs. When I got my knee onto the bottom rung, I was on my way to the second floor.

The blackened window was shut. I found its lock was weak and with upward pressure it gave way. The window open, I turned to wave to Arbuthnott standing with hand to mouth in anticipation. I stepped into a small backroom. A light glimmering under the door warned me that Storey was in the main room. Turning the handle slowly, I edged the door open to where I could see into the room. The redheaded Storey was working by the light of a small lamp that he had set over Margin's safe. The safe door was open, and Storey was looking through sheafs of stamps. Suddenly Storey cursed and threw them to the floor. He stepped to a telephone on Margin's work desk and dialed.

"I'm here," he said. "But I can't find it!" He kicked irritably at a box by his foot. "That was easy to open. Too easy. Makes me think he's got them hidden somewhere in this unholy mess." He looked round at the shelves of boxes and envelopes covering the walls. "It'd take me a year to look through this stuff." He stirred impatiently as he listened to his interlocutor. "Okay, I'll do that." He hung up, looked round the room with disgust, and walked quickly to the door.

I heard him descend the stairs. I waited in the ensuing silence. The fact that Storey had left the light on, the safe open, and the stamps on the floor could mean that he would return. But if he were to return, it would have to be with more information--which he could only get from Winslow Margin who lived two blocks away. That gave me about fifteen minutes.

I went over to the stamps and picked them up off the floor. They looked valuable, but they were not the ones stolen from the Library. The telephone rang, startling me. I put the stamps on the table and let it ring three times before picking up the receiver.

"Glad I caught you," said a male voice. The speaker paused. "Are you all right? Hello!" He paused again and hung up.

I recognized Stavoris's voice. I was badly shaken. At the same time, I tried to imagine where Margin would have put the stamps which he just received and was expecting to get rid of immediately. Storey was right. It was like looking for a needle in a haystack. I stepped to the front door and listened. My eye caught the large mail receptacle attached to the door, and, as if hit by inspiration, I opened the top to find a brown paper parcel inside. Taking it to the light, I opened it. There was a large stamp album in red leather. On the fly leaf was a book plaque with the words "Property of James New." Leafing through the pages, I glimpsed the stamps under neatly printed headings. At least I had one part of New's collection, which indicated that the remainder was not in the store. I put the album back in the brown paper, started for the front door, thought better of it, and went through the back room. As I was stepping out the window, I heard the front door swing open and bang against the wall. I went down the fire escape like a man half my age, dropped to the ground, and tossed the parcel over the fence to Arbuthnott.

"Quick!" I cried. "Run towards Third Avenue."

"I was getting worried," she said.

"Get moving!" I ordered, leaping onto the fence.

She ran out of the parking lot as I climbed clumsily over the fence. She had disappeared into the street before I touched the ground. As I started to run, I turned round to see Storey's head appear at the window. I caught up to Arbuthnott on Third Avenue and hailed a cab.

"Let's go to your place," I said as we got in.

Arbie gave her address to the driver.

"Storey saw me," I gasped between breaths.

"I was having kittens," Arbie said. "You were so long!"

"I heard Storey on the phone," I explained. "After he left, the same guy called again. I picked up the receiver so he knew someone was there. He must have got in touch with Storey about it. But look!" I flicked on the light in the back of the cab. "We've got New's stamps."

"Great!" Arbie said taking the album from the parcel and leafing through it. "Look at these, Rudy! Look how neatly they're arranged. Aren't they beautiful" She stopped at a page marked "United States Airmail."

"Hold it!" I cried, taking back the album. I studied the stamps on the page, all airmail. I turned to the next page--all colorful stamps. When I turned to the third page, we saw the lettering "US Air Mail, 1918, 24 cents." And under this "The Inverted Jenny." But the remainder of the page was blank.

"Gone!" Arbie said. "Oh fucking hell!"

"Old Winslow is a fox," I said. "Trouble is we have to hide these stamps." I switched off the light.

"And we're gonna hide them in my apartment?" Arbie shouted angrily. "I'm in enough trouble with management. I don't need this!"

"I think Storey knows who I am by now," I said. "We could leave them in a luggage box at Grand Central Station."

"Hell, it's all right," Arbie said. "I might as well be one hundred percent involved in this case."

The taxi cruised along the west side of the park and turned into a street in the West 60's.

"Right here, driver," Arbie said.

I paid the fare and followed her into a red-brick apartment house which had no doorman. She found her key, pushed open the inside door and went to the first floor apartment. "You haven't seen my place, have you, Rudy? It's small but cozy. And it's rent-controlled." She turned her key in the apartment door but could not open it. "Rudy!" she cried in shock. She turned the key the other way. "My door is unlocked!" She pushed the door open, turned on the light, and led me into her living room.

The coffee table was overturned, papers were strewn over the floor, her desk drawers were all pulled open. "God, Rudy! I've been robbed!" She ran into her bedroom and came back crying. "The place is a mess! Those bastards!" She flung herself on my shoulder and sobbed.

I held her tightly and looked round the room. "Everything seems to be here," I said. "Television, record player, tape recorder. They must have been looking for something special."

She turned round to look. She walked round examining everything. She blew her nose and went into her bedroom. I examined the front door. Its lock had been picked.

"You're right!" Arbie said, reappearing from the bedroom. "Nothing seems to be missing."

"Let's have some coffee and something to eat," I said. "We've got to think."

"I've got some rice pudding," Arbie said.

"That'll be our dessert, sweetheart."

"Surprise," Arbie said and went into the kitchen.

I leaned in the door and watched her maneuver in the narrow room. "They've got our number," I said. "We can't just sit here like ducks. We've got to go after the big ones."

"What are you saying!" Arbie slammed the kettle on the stove.

"We can't stay with the small fry any longer," I explained. "You were right, Arbie." I went into the living room, looked into the telephone book, and dialed a number.

Arbie went to the door and put the latch chain on. "Who are you calling?"

"Is this Homer Margin? This is Rudyard Mack. I'm in a bit of trouble and I have to see you. I know it's after midnight but it's about the stamp theft." I sensed Homer's irritation and called upon his loyalty to the Library until he agreed reluctantly to our visit within the half-hour.

Arbie brought in the coffee and rice pudding on a tray.

"You're not staying here tonight," I said. "You're coming with me."

"Ah!" Arbie drawled disappointedly. "My bed wasn't touched. I thought we could put New's stamp album under the pillow."

I laughed. "It's too hot to lie under our heads, baby. No, I got an idea. We're going to take it to Homer Margin as soon as we finish this."

"That character! He's not to be trusted!" Arbie cried, tasting the coffee, then said, "Hope the coffee's strong enough. I need an antidote."

I drained my cup. "The sooner we leave here the better." I stood up. "Come on!"

"Oh, screw it!" Arbie gulped down her pudding, took a gulp of coffee, and followed me to the door. "Got the parcel?"

"Damn it!" I said and rushed back to the living room to return with the parcel.

Arbie gave me a look of hopelessness. "You're thinking too hard. And I'm too scared to think."

TWELVE

Homer Margin lived in one of the old, large apartments with high ceilings in the Eighties west of Eighth Avenue. It was still under rent control, otherwise

51

a librarian could not have afforded it. I noted the cost of the taxi ride in my expense book as we took the elevator to the third floor.

Homer was waiting impatiently in the hallway by the elevator. He was wearing pink pajamas, green dressing gown, and brown bedroom slippers. He did not look happy.

"You know Arbuthnott Vine," I said.

"Yes," Homer said stonily. "I know the Union." He turned to lead us into his apartment without the slightest surprise at Arbie's presence.

Arbie winked at me, put up three fingers, and whispered, "We stopped terminations."

"How long are you planning to stay?" Homer asked pushing the apartment door shut behind us.

"Just long enough to get your help," I said pleasantly.

"Then wait in there," he pointed to his living room. "I only have beer." He went to the kitchen.

The walls of the room from floor to ceiling were lined with books. There were books piled on the tables; there were even some books on the floor. When I went to sit down, I had to remove a book from the chair and find room for it on the closest table. Predominantly displayed in a large block frame on one wall were two small pins stuck into a white background. I recognized them as the New York Public Library service pins: ten years and twenty-five years.

Arbie was looking through Ruskin's *Stones of Venice* when Homer reappeared with a tray and three bottles of beer with glasses.

"Luckily I wasn't asleep when you called," Homer said. "I don't answer the telephone after I go to bed." He gave us the beer and sat down with his glass. "Unlike detectives, I guess," he added. He looked even smaller in the evening and his eyes were owlish.

I apologized again for the late hour and explained briefly that our possession of New's stamps had led us into difficulties with the criminal element. "I'm sorry to say this, Homer," I felt I should use his first name because I was drinking Homer's beer in Homer's apartment, "but your brother is mixed up in it."

Homer was taken aback for a moment, then changed his expression. "That doesn't surprise me one bit!" Homer said fiercely. "He's the sort whose blind arrogance can get him into trouble."

"You're right; he's offering to sell back the Postmaster Provisional stamps stolen from the Library," I said.

"Never," Homer winced. "He may be arrogant, but he wouldn't do that. He's not that stupid. He'd never let his name get mixed up in his transactions, let alone get involved in something connected with the New York Public Library."

I sat forward. "Look, Homer, if it is not your brother, then who is it? Are you going to tell me that someone is pretending to be your brother?"

"I don't know, but possibly," Homer said. "He's been in stamps for thirty years. I hate him, but I respect him for his discretion above all else."

"Then, how come he had the James New stamps?" I held up the parcel. "It only follows he took out the Inverted Jenny too."

Homer shook his head. "He just wouldn't handle that. I know my brother."

"A dealer in Buffalo thinks he is capable of crooked deals."

"Dealers are in cut-throat competition!" Homer cried angrily. "They try to outwit one another and out-fox the collector." He picked a book off the floor by his chair and tossed it onto a table. "I don't mean he's one hundred percent honest. Who's honest in that kind of business? But he's not going to blackmail the Library!"

"Okay!" Arbie said suddenly. "But he's in trouble right now. The same guy who wants to kill us is after him."

I put up a cautionary hand. "We don't know if he wants to kill us," I emphasized.

"Yes we do," Arbie said sharply.

Homer was alarmed. "What on earth are you people talking about? Who's trying to kill you? Are you pulling my leg? Shouldn't you have told the police?"

"No," I said. "This whole thing is too involved, and we're not sure of anything at the moment. Until a minute ago, I thought Winslow was the brains behind the theft. Now, after talking to you, I think he may be innocent, or only marginally involved."

"But is he going to be killed?" Homer exclaimed, aghast.

"That's why we're here," I said firmly. "Can you get him over here on some pretense or other?"

"No! I cannot!" Homer said angrily. "We haven't said a word in years. Family dispute."

"But he's your brother, isn't he, you ass?" Arbie cried.

I looked warningly at her, but Homer simply nodded.

"Yes, blood is thicker than water and all that, but I can't call him out of the blue, especially at this time of the night. Be reasonable," Homer protested.

"But his life is in danger!" Arbie shouted.

I arched my eyebrows at Arbie as we waited. Homer looked at me and then at Arbie and then reluctantly went to his telephone.

"I can't guarantee I can convince him he's in danger or to come here now," Homer said dialing Winslow's number while we looked on. He was just about to hang up when Winslow came on the line.

"Hope I didn't disturb you," Homer said a little nervously. He held his hand over the receiver and whispered, "He just got in. Probably making a stamp deal with one of those crooks."

"This is Homer," he said into the receiver. "Yes, I know it's unusual but I'm not very well. I need to see you." He looked questioningly at me. "I'm sorry but if you don't come now it may be too late. It's important, Winslow." His voice was becoming querulous as he nodded excitedly. "No, I'm not pulling your leg. No, I'm not exaggerating. I really need to see you urgently." He paused and then after what seemed like an eternity, he said, "Thanks, brother." He hung up. "Winslow's a man of action," he said, turning to us.

"You'd better get into bed," Arbie laughed.

"Good Heavens! He probably thinks I'm dying or something. You had better do the explaining," Homer retorted. "Winslow is short on humor."

"Runs in the family," Arbie said sarcastically.

"What's she doing here with you?" Homer demanded, annoyed. "What's the Union got to do with the stamps?"

"She's been very helpful," I explained.

"I represent the staff, and it's interested in the theft, particularly when people like you spread rumors that staff is involved," Arbie said caustically.

"I didn't say that!" Homer said defensively.

"Let's leave the quarrel for grievance procedures," I cut in. "We've got to find a way of putting your brother to the test. What do you know about international dealing in stolen stamps?"

"Winslow used to talk about it in the early days." Homer went to a bookshelf, took down "Finn's World Stamp Almanac," and turned to a page he had marked. He pointed to a paragraph as he handed the book to me.

I read, "Winslow Margin, A.P.S. accredited Judge. What's the capital 'I' mean?" I asked.

"International proficiency," Homer smiled. "He's pretty good."

I read: "Czechoslovakia; Germany; British colonies, Straits Settlements; US 1869's, 1920's."

"If Winslow was really considered crooked," Homer said, "the American Philatelic Society would drop him like that!" He snapped his fingers, inadvertently revealing brotherly pride.

"How honest is the A.P.S.?" Arbie asked.

Homer stared blankly at her.

"I see it has a theft committee," I said. "It collects clippings from local newspapers on stamp thefts. It must be used in tracing criminal patterns."

"I've got it!" Arbie jumped to her feet. "Why not ask Winslow about the 1869 inverteds that you saw in his shop?" She paced excitedly up and down. "He's supposed to be an international expert in US 1869's. See if he can claim they weren't stolen from the Library without lying."

"Homer, can you be a lie detector for us?" I asked.

"Oh, I'll know when he's lying, all right," Homer said.

"But we don't know when you're lying," Arbie said, belligerently. "How do we know blood's not thicker than water?"

"Mr. Mack!" Homer looked at me in protest.

"Okay," I said. "I trust you. Don't mind her."

The apartment bell rang.

"I'm too nervous. You'd better answer it," Homer said to me.

Arbie leapt to her feet. "I've got it," she said striding to the door.

She returned with Winslow Margin looking very concerned. Winslow stopped short in surprise, and his face registered a series of questions such as why are you out of bed? who are these people? why are you looking so healthy?

"I'm not sick," Homer admitted. He could hardly look at Winslow. "But I had to get you here by hook or by crook. Your life is in danger, Winslow. Ask these people."

"What?" Winslow glared in disgust. He took off his hat with a brusque, angry gesture and gave it to Arbie. "Are you playing one of your stupid jokes?" He turned and saw me for the first time. He did not seem to recognize me as the man who once visited his shop and asked about stamps.

"This is Rudyard Mack, the library detective," Homer said. "I'll get us some beer, excuse me." He went into the kitchen.

Winslow ignored the introduction. He still seemed not to remember me.

"Do you know that this parcel was in the mail box at your store?" I asked breaking the silence and handing him New's album in the brown paper wrapping.

Winslow, frowning, took out the red leather volume, sat down, and began looking closely at the stamps in it.

"The owner was murdered for it," I said casually, watching him closely. "How did it get addressed to your store?"

"Never saw it!" Winslow said sternly. "How did you get it, did you say?"

"It was found in your mail box tonight," I repeated, asserting the tone of the omniscient detective. "When I examined the album, the Inverted Jenny was missing. It was the one stolen from the Library."

"So I heard," Winslow said, thoroughly engrossed in the contents of the album. He took out an eye glass and continued to examine the stamps closely. "Anyone could have dropped this into my post box from outside the door," he acknowledged.

"There's a redhead named Storey who thinks you've got the Inverted Jenny," I said. "I think he called at your home earlier this evening."

"Is he a dealer?" Winslow asked without looking up.

"He's a killer!" Arbie said emphatically.

Winslow pretended not to hear her and continued studying the stamps. "Whoever stole this album knew nothing about stamps. There's a fortune here. There's even the world's first stamp: the Great Britain Penny Blue of 1840."

I cleared my throat and took the plunge. "Do you own some U S Postmaster Provisionals?"

"Wish I did," Winslow said, closing the album and handing the stamps back. He seemed unfazed by my question.

"Someone saying he was you offered to sell back the Provisionals stolen from the Library," I said quietly. "I've been given the job of dealing with you."

"I can't deal," Winslow smiled for the first time. His smile was similar to Homer's smile which occurred just as rarely.

Homer returned with four beers and glasses which he handed round. He showed a deference bordering on respect to his brother, of which I had not thought him capable.

"You were ready to deal with 1869 Inverted Centers," I smiled.

"Yes," Winslow nodded and poured his beer. "I recall your visit."

"You are aware that some were stolen from the Library," I said flatly.

"I was." Winslow sipped his beer and touched his mustache with his fingertips. He was plumper and stockier than Homer. "I received the stamp which I showed you from an unimpeachable source, the Corporation Internationale des Negociants en Timbres-Postes in Brussels. I'm sure that it was not stolen."

"But," Arbie intervened, "don't you auction stamps when they get that valuable?"

"Not always," Winslow said. "Collectors like to sell privately. Sometimes they make a swap."

"Who could be setting you up, brother?" Homer asked suddenly.

"No idea," Winslow shrugged. "The business has been getting nastier since the high inflation, but it sounds extreme for one of my competitors to do." He spoke directly to Homer as if there had never been a disagreement between them.

"Who owns the 1869 inverted?" I asked.

"Don't know," Winslow took a long swallow of beer. "But I believe, one of the Corporation members. The secretary sent it to me."

"Will you find out for me?"

"Of course," Winslow nodded and yawned.

"Meanwhile, for tonight, don't go back to your apartment," I warned.

"Are you serious?" Winslow expostulated with a look of astonishment, and when he saw that I was serious, he shook his head, "I didn't think it could come to this."

"Afraid it has, Winslow," Homer said. "You can stay here. I'll get the couch ready."

"We'll help you take the books off it," Arbie said going to the couch in the corner.

Winslow wanted to decline, but he hesitated, thinking no doubt of the late hour, then gave Homer a grateful look.

"Hold onto these stamps for now, will you?" I said, giving the parcel to Homer. "Hide them somewhere until I tell you to turn them over to the police." I turned to Winslow. "Once the news is out that they've been found, you'll be safe."

"Make sure it's on all the television and radio stations," Arbie warned. "That idiot redhead won't hear it otherwise." She held up the Ruskin book. "Can I borrow this?"

Homer grimaced. "Okay, but return it!"

"Meanwhile it's almost three," I said looking at my watch. "Let's go, Arbie."

Homer, effusively expressing his thanks and obviously happy that he had broken the ice with his brother, escorted us to the door.

"Did he tell the truth?" I asked.

Homer, beaming, nodded. "I'm beholden to you for making this happen."

I said to Arbie in the elevator, "That leaves us on Square One."

Arbie yawned, threw her arms about me, and set her head sleepily on my shoulder.

I put my arm about her, "Come on," and led her into the street where, after walking for a minute, I was lucky to get a cab on Eighth Avenue.

Arbie dozed on my shoulder on the ride to my place. I tried to imagine who was behind the sale of the 1869 Inverted Center. It was already Saturday morning. Nothing could be done until Monday. But it would be the first big clue. I had a hunch it could lead to the murderer of James New. I shouted. The taxi was going beyond the apartment entrance. The cabby looked as sleepy as we did.

"Rudy!" Arbie exclaimed as she watched me pay. "Look at your dirty hands!"

I saw black smears over my palms and shirt cuffs in the lamplight.

"Must have been Margin's window. I need a shower like nobody's business."

As we approached the entrance, a slim redheaded man stepped out from behind a bush beside the sidewalk. He pointed a revolver straight at us.

"Good evening, Mister and Misses," he said jocularly. "Vine alias Mack, I presume."

Arbie was shocked rigid.

"Mr. Storey alias Macdonald, I presume," I said coolly. The taxi had driven off. The street was deserted.

Storey pushed the gun into my chest, reached inside my coat and pulled out my pistol which he put in his own pocket. "Get into that car, you skinny crud!"

A car glided to a stop by the curb, and the back door swung open. I helped Arbie by the arm as we climbed in. Storey slammed the door, looked around him, and got into the front. His thin, mustached friend drove off. I caught a vision of the East River--wide, black and swift.

THIRTEEN

Storey sat with his left arm bent over the seat back and his right holding the gun over it. Slouching back in the seat, I tried to look relaxed.

"I haven't got the encyclopedia," I said.

"Smart guy, aren't you, Mack?" Storey grinned. "Go east on 14th," he told his companion. We stopped for a red light.

"We don't have the Inverted Jenny either," I said.

"Right to the point," Storey grinned again.

"We don't know who stole James New's stamps, and we don't know where they are," I rode the lie piggy-back on the truth with conviction, or so I thought.

"Okay," Storey nodded seriously. "Then what were you doin' in the stamp store?"

"Same as you!" Arbie said shrilly. "Pisshead!"

Storey pointed the gun at her. "Keep this nutty woman quiet or I'll blast her."

We were moving again. No cops anywhere. Just a few cars and some deadbeats holding onto the buildings along 14th Street.

"What's more," I continued, "we know that you don't know where the Jenny is. We don't know why you want it."

"A lot of 'dunnos' I'm hearing," Storey said. "Do you believe it?" he asked his companion.

His companion said nothing.

"Since we both don't know," Storey said, "and I believe you--otherwise you'd have returned the Jenny to the Library--since we both don't know, why don't we work together to find out?" He nudged the gun a little closer to me meaningfully.

We were on the East River Drive heading south.

"And if we don't?" I asked concealing my surprise at his offer of cooperation.

57

"If you're not with me, you're against me," Storey grinned. "Right?"

We pulled off to the side and parked across from the East River Park.

"What's your game?" I asked, indicating that I was tired of the play-acting. "Who do you work for?"

It was Storey's turn to look taken aback. "That'll have to be a 'dunno' for the time being," he smiled. "I know that you know I'm in the insurance business. In fact, you know too much about me. With that kind of knowledge we should be working closer together. It'd be a real pity if we don't." He paused, "Otherwise..." his voice trailed off as he drew his hand across his throat. Just then the car stopped. "Let's get out," he said. He got out of the car and opened the back door for us. Still training his gun on us, he motioned to the pedestrian bridge. As we walked to it, Storey called over his shoulder to his companion. "There's a phone on the next street."

We walked over the bridge into the park lit dimly by the lights from the roadway. Arbie held my arm tightly.

"Keep going--straight to the river," Storey ordered.

I was too apprehensive to talk, but my mind was racing. I could not try to escape for fear that Arbie would be hurt. The bushes at the sides of the path seemed inviting, but presently we were on the lawn under the trees and onto the walk alongside the river. Storey motioned to us to sit on a bench and perched on the end of it next to Arbie.

Storey cleared his throat. "Fact is, we both want the same thing--we want the stamps back, right?"

"Back for the Library, not for the same reasons as you," I said scornfully.

"We're not so far apart, you know," Storey said agreeably. "New's death brought us closer together, you might say. When we find the stamps, we can come to an arrangement."

"Who do you think killed New?" Arbie asked, her curiosity getting the better of her.

Storey flared in anger. "This bird asks the stupidest questions. Tell her to shut up! Do you hear? Shut up!"

I put my hand on Arbie's knee as if to calm her, and I began to play Storey's game. "How can we work together if we haven't got a clue to work on?" I asked quietly, as if coming around to his way of thinking. "If you have a clue, tell me."

"You agree then?" Storey said. "We're partners?" He looked closely at me.

I nodded.

"Look," Storey warned, "if you turn us in, you'd be finished off, d'ya understand? You won't know when or where it's coming from. There's no welching on this agreement."

"No welching," I said in agreement.

Arbie was about to say something, but I quickly pressed my hand on her shoulder.

"That's better," Storey said, looking amused at us. "Women should be seen and not heard."

Arbie gritted her teeth.

58

"The way I see it," Storey started to sound absurdly confidential and philosophical, "another group that works the stamp racket killed New for some guy who found out that New had the Inverted Jenny."

I looked at the lights of Brooklyn across the river as a sense of relief spread throughout my body.

"New just wanted the Jenny. He didn't want any of the rest," Storey continued. "My boss got rid of the rest easy enough."

"That's important," I said. "Who did he sell the rest to?"

"They're in Europe, that's all he'll tell me," Storey said with an undertone of resentment that I was quick to notice. "Besides," Storey smirked, "you know I didn't get all the stamps I stole." He was referring to the stamps in the linings of the last two volumes of the encyclopedia which I caught Berney trying to smuggle out of the Library through a stack window in order to deliver them to him.

"Forget them," I said. "They're not part of our agreement."

Storey laughed in a low-voiced cackle. "You can't be bought for sixty thousand?"

I ignored the question. "Where does this so-called group work out of?" I asked.

"Oh, they're all over. But I think Brussels is their Headquarters."

I nodded.

The thin, mustached man appeared on the walkway. He had completed his telephone call. He made a thumbs-up sign. Dawn streaked across the sky.

"Okay," Storey said, "the boss says you can live." He smiled and put his gun away. "You tell us what you find out, and we'll tell you what we find out. Okay?" He gave me my gun back and stood up.

"Okay," I said returning my gun to its holster. Storey's companion had disappeared.

"You want a ride back?" Storey asked.

"We want to watch the sunrise," I said pointing to the light in the eastern sky.

"Nothing like romance," Storey laughed and quickly walked away.

I kept my arm about Arbie for a long time as we sat silently watching the sun climb out from behind Brooklyn.

"Maybe," Arbie said finally, "we're getting too involved."

"One thing," I said. "We have to have whoever is behind Storey put away if we want to live normally."

"Don't say 'put away' like that!" Arbie said. "It makes me think of what almost happened to us."

In the distance, a police officer patrolled the riverside looking over the railing every so often to see into the water.

"We'd better go," I suggested.

"But no taxi," Arbie pleaded. "Please. I've got to walk off this terrible feeling of anxiety or I'll never fall asleep."

We walked arm-in-arm, lost in thought, occasionally suggesting what we could do next, until we greeted the doorman and gained the safety of my apartment.

"Get your shower while I rustle us up some breakfast," Arbie said. "Then we'll make love."

"Sounds pretty good," I kissed her. I felt a twinge of recognition of matrimonial order.

I started the shower, went to the phone and called Homer.

"Homer? Look, hang onto those stamps. Don't do anything until I tell you. It's important; I want to look at them again."

Before I stepped into the shower, I noticed it was eight o'clock. When I got out, it was eight-thirty. Arbie was impatiently waiting at the kitchen table.

"I hope you left water for me," she said.

I put on the top of my pajamas. "Damn! I almost forgot. They wanted me in this morning. I'll call Bugofsky's secretary." I went to the phone.

"It's Saturday, for God's sake!" Arbie called after me.

Bugofsky answered. I was so surprised that I had trouble speaking.

"Where the hell are you? You're supposed to be in here! Now!" Bugofsky was in an uncontrollable fury. "A guy terrified a reader in the reading room yesterday. And you were in Buffalo! Christ in Heaven, get over here fast! The morning newspaper's got a hold of it. Every body's asking 'Where the fuck is the security?' 'He's in Buffalo!' God-damn it, Mack, if you want to keep your job, you get over here now!" He slammed down the receiver.

I went back to eat a quick breakfast. "You'll have to sleep alone, sweetheart; that was Bugofsky. He wants me right away."

Arbie pouted. "Some day Sharkey and me are gonna have a real knock 'em down, drag-it-out showdown." She took a long drink of coffee.

FOURTEEN

When I got to Bugofsky's office, there was a large delegation of women standing in both the inner and outer rooms. I recognized some of them from their high boots as members of the writing fraternity which pursued research in various rooms of the Library. Bugofsky stood at his gracious, debonair best, smiling handsomely amongst them. He was listening and nodding attentively to what a small group was shouting at him. When he saw me, a hard glint came into his smiling eyes. Excusing himself with little bows of the head, he detached himself from the ladies, seized me by the arm and took me across the anteroom into the assistant business manager's office.

Although we worked in the same department, I encountered the assistant only rarely. Small and retiring by nature, he was dominated by Bugofsky who consigned him to his office to do the paperwork. Bugofsky gestured with his thumb for him to leave.

"Keep those bags happy," he growled.

When the assistant scampered out, Bugofsky sat in his chair, took out a cigar and lit it. I waited for an angry torrent of words, but Bugofsky spoke in a moderate tone.

"Mental patient, just released, stabbed a man reading in the North Reading Hall. In the face and neck. No provocation. I've tightened security at the entrance. We have to spot these guys before they can do any harm. You work on it, Rudyard."

"Right," I said, wondering what other problems he was going to pile onto me.

"It's stirred up a hornet's nest here," Bugofsky said. "So get to it!"

As I started to go, Bugofsky asked, "Where's the sixty thousand bucks?" He smiled cunningly. "For the encyclopedia?"

"No deal," I said glumly.

Bugofsky looked disappointed and then shouted, "You're no good, Mack! Get the hell out of here!"

I checked an impulse to shout back, but I gave him a hard stare which took him aback somewhat.

"Oh! I almost forgot," he said huskily. "Betterton wants to see you."

From pillar to post, I thought, as I walked the marble halls to Betterton's office. I found the door open to President Stavoris's office and Stavoris, Anders, Betterton and Detective Buckle seated at a conference table.

"Ah, here he is. Come join us," Betterton called. "We want to hear from you. How is the search progressing?" He gestured with his long arm for me to sit by him as if he were signaling for a forward pass.

"Nothing definite yet," I said, stifling a yawn and beginning to feel my lack of sleep.

"Perhaps you'll have something for us soon, will you, Mr. Mack?" Stavoris said hopefully. "Inspector Buckle here tells us that it looks as if we shall never be able to trace our stamps. He thinks we should take the insurance money and forget the whole business."

"And what do you think, sir?" I asked.

"Well, we were rather hoping you would provide us with the answer to that, Rudyard," Betterton said.

I looked at Buckle fully aware that he resented me for mixing in police business. "Since one man has already been murdered because of the Inverted Jenny, we'd be doing everyone a favor if we got it back."

Buckle chuckled, highly amused. "You wouldn't know this, Mack, but an international stamp theft is such a maze that once you enter into it, you'll never get out. It'll cost the police department more money than it's worth. I'm speaking from experience."

"Give me another week," I said to Stavoris. "I'll give you an answer then."

Stavoris looked at the others and then nodded at me. "I think we can do that," Stavoris smiled. "Though it seems you are indispensable here in the Library."

"Mr. Bugofsky," Betterton explained in mellifluous tones, "has requested that you be taken off the case. But I think we can manage another week."

I caught a look of disdain in Buckle's fat face. The conversation switched to the stabbing incident. I listened while Buckle complained about the emptying of the mentally sick into the streets of Manhattan. I tried to compare the voice of Stavoris to the voice which I had heard over Winslow Margin's telephone. There was the same heavy cadence.

Stavoris's secretary came into the room and winsomely apologized for interrupting. "Mr. Mack has a call."

I took the call at her desk in the outer office. It was Frank Aragon, the dandified stamp dealer, calling from Buffalo.

"I've been transferred all over the Library looking for you," he complained and then announced brightly, "I got some good information about Mr. New. He was killed by a ring operating out of Belgium. It's believed that his stamps are in Brussels."

"Give me a name," I said.

"The ring is called the Masonic Stamp Center," Aragon lowered his voice to a confidential tone. "I don't know the names of the principals. I'll keep making inquiries, but, you know, I have to be careful."

"You're doing a good job, Frank. When are you coming down?"

"I'll see you Monday," Aragon said. "For lunch?"

"Come to the Library at one," I said.

When I re-entered Stavoris's office, the meeting was breaking up.

"Inspector Buckle has promised to give you any help you may need, Mr. Mack," Stavoris said.

"Feel free to call," Buckle said magnanimously.

I muttered my thanks and felt Betterton's arm encircle my shoulders. "Let's talk privately, Rudyard. We'll use your office, Amos, if that is agreeable with you?"

"Certainly," Anders said. "It's not very tidy, but ah! it's quiet."

Anders's office was large and oblong. Unlike Stavoris's richly decorated room, it had the look of the poorly-paid clerk: carpetless floor, sparsely furnished, as if to present the image of poverty to the library grievants and unionists who met there with the Director. Betterton signaled for me to sit at the long table where staff demands were thrashed out and evaded.

"I'll come to the point," Betterton said. "We in the administration of the Library, indeed, just as in the administration of any corporation of this country, have a responsibility to our fellow administrators and to the well-running of the Library. We have to be circumspect in all that we say and do with respect to library business." He paused to study the effect of his words.

I looked blankly at him. "I understand, sir."

"We have the confidence in one another that whatever we say will not be repeated outside of our circle." Henry Betterton looked grave. "If one of us breaks the faith and talks too openly, we all lose that sense of confidence. The institution cannot function. It breaks down."

I imagined the high white walls and the tall windows of the New York Public Library beginning to crumble.

"In this regard," Betterton continued in a monotone, "in this respect, the President, the Director and I myself heard some rather incredible reports about you and your associations."

I groaned inwardly as Betterton paused for emphasis.

"I am alluding to you and Miss Vine of course," Betterton said suddenly. "I don't know how close your association is, but, for the sake of precaution, it should not be continued."

62

"It's not close, sir," I lied. "I just know her as the Union President."

"You were seen together at a coffee shop near here." Betterton frowned. "One of our senior programmers reported it to us right away. We've been keeping an eye on you, Rudyard, and found that you and she are too frequently together for our liking."

"Well, uh...," I searched for an appropriate response.

"Miss Vine is a very dangerous person. She is a socialist! We can tell that from the Union Newsletters. Even her union leaders downtown disown her. Thank God, we can deal with them directly on important matters. She actually thinks she can speak for the staff!"

"The staff elected her," I reminded him. "It didn't elect the union officers downtown."

"The staff made a mistake!" Betterton worked himself into a temper. "It will be corrected the next time around."

"I find her honest, straightforward and pleasant to talk to, sir," I said, feeling I had to defend Arbie. "Besides, she never asks me about library business, and we never talk shop."

"She doesn't?" Betterton looked very surprised and then smiled. "No, I don't suppose she would. But, please, Rudyard, be careful not to be seen with her. Lord knows, we're in enough trouble as it is! What, with all these robberies! By the way, congratulations on finding the encyclopedia. I'll look forward to your report on it."

"When I get a chance," I said, getting up as Betterton stood and took my hand in a strong athletic grip.

"Remember, Rudyard, stay clear of the library union--it's poison. And if you add that pretty woman, the poison is fatal."

I laughed appreciatively. I reached the marble hallway with a feeling of relief that surprised me by its intensity. I glanced at my watch. An hour and a half working hours remaining in the morning. I was dog-tired from being up all night. Damn Bugofsky! I had only a week to find the missing stamps. I decided to skip the patrolling of the reading rooms. After all, the odds that another mental patient would strike the Library so soon after the first were impossibly high. I raced down the stairs to my office, scooped up a metal box, a camera, and a small tripod from my bottom drawer and glided out the 40th Street exit while furtively looking round for signs of Bugofsky. I caught a taxi and gave Homer Margin's west side address.

FIFTEEN

I met Homer carrying two heavy bags of groceries into the hallway of his building.

"Winslow and I talked all morning," Homer said. "I think he's feeling a bit restless."

"He'll be fine after he hears my news," I said as Homer pressed the elevator button. "Anyway I should think he'd want your company after a ten-year absence."

63

"Let us rejoice that we're even talking," Homer said.

When we reached the apartment, Winslow opened the door with an exclamation of surprise at seeing me.

"Got the stamps?" I asked, all business-like.

"Just been looking at them," Winslow said leading me to the living room. "It's a fabulous collection!"

"Right!" I opened my tin box and brought out the instruments. "Open that ink pad and spread out that blotting paper. I want the prints of the forefinger, second finger, and thumb of both you and Homer." I opened New's stamp album to the blank paper from which the Inverted Jenny had been lifted, sprinkled black graphic powder over the page, and agitated it until a number of prints appeared; most of them at the top and bottom of the page but two near the center. I tapped on the reverse side of the page to get rid of the unnecessary powder, then set up my tripod over the page, inserted the camera and photographed the prints.

"Here are ours," Homer said handing me the blotting paper.

After I photographed the prints of the Margin brothers, I put the album, the blotting paper, and other paraphernalia into my box and gathered my camera equipment and turned to Winslow. "Ever heard of the Masonic Stamp Center, a secret brotherhood of stamp thieves?"

Winslow smiled knowingly. "It works out of Brussels. But I've never heard it described like that. Its members are powerful men." He frowned. "By the way, I called my contact at the Corporation Internationale des Negociants about that 1869 inverted center. He'll find out the owner's name and call me back."

"Good!" I said. "You should be all right when word gets round that I have New's stamp album."

"Will I?" Winslow asked nervously.

I saw for the first time that Winslow was actually a very frightened man. "The men who want the album," I said reassuringly, "should know that I have it which means that they should be after me."

"That word 'should' covers a lot of ground," Homer interjected, allying himself in sympathy with his brother. "How can Winslow be sure?"

"Be careful for a day or two," I warned and walked towards the door.

Homer sped ahead of me and opened it. "I didn't mean to be critical," he said apologetically, "but my brother has been under a strain."

"See what you can find for me on the Masonic Stamp Center," I said firmly. "That's the best way you can help your brother."

I saw a glint in Homer's eye at the suggestion of useful research. I thought, as I reached the street, that I might well have a line-up of its members now that Homer was prepared to ferret them out.

I found a note from Arbuthnott at my apartment:

Darling--Gone to apt. Called police about burglar. See you. xx Arbie.

I developed the film while I ate lunch. Some of the prints at the bottom and top of the page had come from the Margin brothers, myself, and possibly two or three others. But the two prints in the center of the page belonged to none of us. In lifting the Inverted Jenny, the thief had pressed the page with his thumb and second finger. They were not New's prints because prints older than three days could not be found by the powder method. No, whoever these prints belonged to took the Jenny and tried to frame Winslow Margin!

I put the findings carefully away in a cabinet, went to bed, and fell into a deep sleep. My telephone awakened me, seemingly immediately, though my watch told me that three hours had passed. It was Storey calling. He was sitting with Winslow Margin in Winslow's apartment. He was about to scramble Winslow's brains when Winslow happened to mention that I had New's stamps.

"But not the Jenny," I yawned. "Go home, I'm working on it."

"You better not double-cross us," Storey warned and hung up.

I awoke at ten o'clock and thought for a moment before I remembered it was evening. I made a copy of the two unknown fingerprints, wrote a note to Detective Buckle asking him to identify them and put them into an envelope. I called Arbuthnott.

"I just woke up," she said, "and I was thinking how marvelous it would be if you took us out to dinner."

I called by for her, and we walked to a restaurant in the West Seventies. The warmer weather of approaching summer had brought out the young in force. The spontaneity of the crowds and the night lights in the glass-walled restaurants seemed to pluck us out of the sordid world of murder and theft into an oasis of gaiety. Our conversation leaped to subjects that we were unaware the other knew or was interested in: literature, painting, music, and our common interest in politics. Our talk carried us through dinner and off to the West End Cafe where we sat hand-in-hand, contentedly sipping drinks and listening to a jazz combo.

"Well, well, if it ain't Mr. Mack," a male voice said, jarring us from a relaxed mood.

We turned to see the black features and white goatee of Berney senior grinning down at us.

"Edgar Berney's father," I announced to Arbie and smiled at Berney senior. "How's Edgar?"

"Sit down, please, Mr. Berney," Arbie insisted.

"Okay," Berney senior stroked his goatee and sat beside me. "He's doin' fine. Out in another week, maybe. How ya doin'?"

"Striking out," I said.

Berney laughed and clapped his hands. "That's cause you're barkin' up the wrong tree."

"Do you know the right tree?"

"Maybe I do, maybe I don't," Berney senior grinned again, trying to look mysterious.

The combo took a break. Students broke into gales of laughter somewhere.

"I make a little in this place here and there," Berney senior said looking round at the tables. "Tossing pennies you might say," he giggled.

"How much is it worth?" I asked, amused.

"Don't want to hold you up, Mr. Mack. You pay me what you think it's worth."

I finished off my whisky.

"Well, let's see," Berney senior huddled closer, his unshaven face brushing my cheek. "The man, Stavoris. He came to see Edgar." He rounded his eyes. "That's something, ain't it? The president of the Library coming to see a technical assistant! So I kind a' listened in unobtrusive-like. And they talked about the stamps. Postmaster Provisionals. The man said he knew that Edgar had them. Edgar said no. My son was telling it truthfully. Then the man went out and came right back with a white man called Macdonald. Edgar got excited and started stutterin'. Seems that Macdonald claims Edgar had the stamps. Edgar called for me; I got the nurse, and we got them out a' there."

"That's not worth much," I said, pretending indifference.

"Wait! That's not all," Berney senior wiped his lips with his forearm. "Stavoris handed me this letter, Mr. Mack. It's a xerox, see."

Dear President Stavoris, The Postmaster Provisional stamps have now been placed with one of your staff members, Edgar Berney. We are dealing no longer through Winslow Margin. Please arrange to make our agreed-upon payment to Mr. Berney. Yours, Hippolyte de Leon

"Must be a practical joke," I said putting it in my pocket. "Someone is framing Edgar."

"The man wants me to search our house for those stamps," Berney senior said with amusement and stood up.

I offered him a ten-dollar bill.

"If that letter leads you to the stamps," Berney senior said, taking it casually, "I ought to get a bigger share, right?"

I watched him walk away, swaying between the tables and turned to Arbie who had read the letter over my shoulder. We were both non-plussed. "Why didn't Stavoris ask me to approach Edgar Berney?" I puzzled.

"Good question," Arbie said. "Also why did he go in person to see Edgar and why did he bring Storey along?--to scare the shit out of Edgar?"

"Whoever this de Leon is, he knows about Edgar," I said. "Whereas I thought only Storey and we knew about him."

"Maybe Edgar really does have the Provisionals," Arbie said.

"No, he doesn't." I looked round carefully and whispered in Arbie's ear, "I have the Postmaster Provisionals."

"You!" Arbie mouthed in surprise.

"I found them in the inside lining of the covers of those last two volumes of *Baker's Encyclopedia*. They never left the Library."

"My God!" Arbie looked round-eyed. "Glad you finally told your partner something," she added with exasperation. "Come on, let's go home. The place is getting creepy. Tomorrow's Sunday and we can sleep late."

SIXTEEN

Before I left for work on Monday, I told Arbie about Henry Betterton's warning that I stay away from her. We agreed to be discreet.

"Someone might like to see me get the ax," I said, "before we solve this case."

My secretary said that Bugofsky wanted to see me right away. She was plump with a high-pitched voice that grated on me first thing in the morning. It made me want to rebel against authority and ignore Bugofsky. I sat at my desk and scanned photocopied request slips for the books on stamps for the name 'Hippolyte de Leon.' I found no name resembling it; there was, however, one reader from Brussels--'K. Vanderlyne.' Vanderlyne had left blank the line requesting "School or Business." I came across Stavoris's name again and puzzled over it. It was hard to believe that President Stavoris had anything to do with the theft when he seemed so eager to recover the stamps.

The telephone rang. It was Bugofsky.

"Good morning," I sang.

"Cut the 'good' crap," Bugofsky growled. "It's a hell of a morning. What have you done about the stamps? Everybody's asking about them."

"I'm working on it," I said calmly.

"We haven't got much time. They're going to give up on this department. I don't want that to happen, Rudyard. They may start cutting us. You'll be the first to go."

"I'm working on it," I repeated.

"Stavoris wants you to check out a reader name of 'Hippolyte de Leon.' Sounds like a commie to me."

"I'll do that," I said. The name 'K. Vanderlyne' intrigued me more, although I had no idea why it should.

"Get out of your office, Rudyard, and get on the floor. We're opening up to the weirdoes!"

Bugofsky regarded anyone who read a book as weird. I thought of the dispossessed and the insane who followed the rush of eager readers into the Library when its doors were opened. Every so often I spent an hour or two plotting their movements about the building. I sized up the cast of characters so that I could assess the likelihood of disruption in service during the day. Also, I had to keep after the guards to check the wastepaper baskets for bombs.

"Hey, Mr. Mack!" an excited cry sounded in the corridor, and Homer strode into my office, alarm spread all over his face. "They almost killed poor Winslow! Did you know that?" he asked, white-faced, as he shut the door.

"Did Storey hurt him?"

"Well, no," Homer admitted, "but that redheaded ruffian frightened him out of his skin."

"But he's still in his skin, isn't he?" I said matter-of-factly. "Storey's bark is worse than his bite."

Homer stepped back with a blank look. "I don't think that's funny, especially after all the hard work I've been doing for you. It was just sheer luck that we persuaded Storey to call you to vouch that we did not have the Jenny."

"Sorry," I smiled. "I have confidence in Winslow's recuperative powers. He's more resilient than you give him credit for. What have you found out about the Masonic Stamp Center?"

"I found only one reference on it--in a Zurich newspaper dated about a year ago," Homer said. He seemed impressed by its clandestine operation. "Swiss police discovered a stamp-printing operation of a very sophisticated nature. And when they traced its lines of communication, they found it was linked with Los Angeles, Honolulu, Valparaiso, Hong Kong, Brussels, New York and other places I forget."

"Sort of a trading route for stamps?" I suggested.

"Oh yes!" Homer brightened. "Not just for their counterfeit stamps but for stolen stamps. Apparently the police found part of a collection stolen from a German dealer."

"Then that's it!" I said excitedly. I was onto the right track at last.

"Look!" Homer pulled a paper from his pocket. "I xeroxed the article for you."

"It's in German," I said disappointedly.

"Yes, but I've underlined the name of the police officer who was in charge of the investigation--Peter Zins. You can at least read that!"

I looked sharply at him. "Okay, Homer, you've done a good job. Now, it's vital that you don't say a word about this to anyone."

Homer nodded and departed, looking pleased.

Switzerland was about six hours ahead of New York time-wise so, I figured, glancing at my watch, it would be 4.50 in the afternoon in Zurich. By good luck, the long distance operator located Peter Zins at the police H.Q. in Zurich. He spoke English and had heard of the New York Public Library stamp theft.

"I huf data on de Masonic Stamp Center," he said crisply. "It seems reasonable de stamps went to Brussels radder dan Zurich. A moment, please." He left the telephone to consult his files. "Hello, Mr. Mack?" Zins continued in his flat, expressionless manner. "We huf reports on stamp activity. Dere are offers to sell American stamps circulating in our big centers of Europe."

Since Zins paused, I asked, "Hear anything about the Inverted Jenny?"

"Not exactly," Zins said. "Radder of inverted center stamps. Dey huf de date 1869."

"Are they being sold from Brussels," I asked scarcely able to believe my good luck in confirming the center for the theft.

"Yes! That's where it's at, as you Americans say," Zins said, humor creeping into his voice.

"Can you give me any names who might be involved?"

"I'll look into de madder and send a report on my findings, yah?" Zins assured me. "De trouble is, dere is a maze of respectable people collecting stamps and belonging to dese organizations. Only some are criminals."

"I just need their American contact," I said and almost asked him about K. Vanderlyne but sensed my request would sound like random guessing that no professional detective would engage in.

"We'll keep watch here," Zins said amicably. "Good luck!"

I tried to think. The thieves took the stamps to Brussels where they had the outlets for selling them to collectors, both honest and dishonest. One of their outlets went through Winslow Margin. I thought Winslow was honest. No

68

doubt there were dishonest outlets in America. But more important I had to find the inlets--the men who funneled the stolen stamps to Brussels in the first place.

I had a hunch that the Inverted Jenny was a main reason for the theft, at least, it seemed to be the reason for New's murder. Possibly the other stamps, aside from their great value, were stolen as a sort of cover and were being circulated around as decoys to fool the police away from whoever had the Inverted Jenny.

The person who probably could answer my questions was Storey's mysterious "boss." I hesitated to pin that appellation on Library President Stavoris, although Stavoris employed Storey in his Continental Insurance Company and seemed to have taken Storey into his confidence in tracking down the stolen stamps. Yet I was sure that Stavoris knew Storey only as Macdonald and remained ignorant of Storey's criminal connections. Stavoris would never risk consorting with a criminal; he had worked his way into the upper echelons of the American business establishment with too much effort to allow the slightest suggestion of criminality spoil his reputation. Despite Arbie's warnings, I thought Stavoris, Betterton and the other trustees were too dedicated to the public good to have become involved in the petty theft of rare stamps from the public domain. No, the crime was the result of an obsession. Whoever was Storey's boss knew who the obsessed one was. But the boss was keeping Storey in the dark possibly because of Storey's business connection with Stavoris and the fear that Storey might betray him. Also, the thought crossed my mind that Storey's boss could have been pushing both Storey and me in pursuit of the Inverted Jenny all the while knowing that we would never find it and that our failure would convince everyone concerned to give up the search. Storey's boss was keeping control over me by having Storey watch me. Moreover, if by chance I discovered who had the Inverted Jenny, I could be killed by either Storey or one of his criminal colleagues. And what was worse, by involving Arbie, I may have made her life worthless too.

Arbie was becoming dearer to me each day. Her naturalness and spunkiness were qualities I admired, but her readiness to stand with me in danger was what most endeared her to me. I had not expected it from her because our politics and general attitude were so different; I had expected a radical like her to put me off as someone who was hopelessly mired in the superstitions of the middle ages. And what I found more surprising was that she came from a middle-class family which had had its moments in New England history, whereas I had regarded her as someone with a background from the working class or from an ancestry of small shopkeepers. That she could like an undistinguished, middle-aged goof like me was amazing. A tide of sentimentality swept over me, and I began to picture her lying naked awash in sexual desire.

"Hullo! I'm too early, aren't I?" Frank Aragon, the dandified stamp collector from Buffalo, stuck his head round the door. "But they told me I'd find you here now, so I came along, on the chance you might be free. Hope you don't mind."

I jumped up and greeted him warmly. I had forgotten I was to meet him. "You timed your arrival just right to suit me, Frank," I said, actually regretting the abrupt end to my sexual reverie.

"I looked at the front hall where you used to keep the stamps," Aragon said brightly. "When will they put them back on view for stamp lovers like me, do you think?" He smiled. He was looking dapper in a red sports coat and white tie.

I took him to a restaurant on 39th Street where one could eat at a leisurely pace and talk.

"The rise in the price of gold can mean a rise in the price of stamps. James New's collection almost doubled its value in the past week," I said as an opener.

"I'll say!" Aragon agreed. "Whoever has them will want to unload them before the price falls."

"Who was behind the theft?" I asked casually but coming to the point at once.

"Appears that it's a clique of wealthy stamp collectors in Belgium who barter and sell stolen stamp collections. In these days that's a billion dollar business," Aragon replied.

"But they didn't kill James New to get his collection, did they?"

"I think James New belonged to their group--loosely affiliated that is, so the story goes," Aragon said. "He double-crossed them somehow. At any rate, Winslow Margin sells stamps for them to the American market."

"Ever heard of Hippolyte de Leon?" I asked suddenly, referring to the man who claimed that Berney had the Postmaster Provisionals.

Aragon thought for a moment, brushed back his thinning hair and said, "Hippolyte de Leon. Wait a moment, I think I've seen that name as a by-line on articles in philately magazines. I assume it's a pseudonym."

"Good. Ever heard of K. Vanderlyne?" This mysterious name on the library request slip had been nagging me.

Aragon looked startled. "Why, he's a Belgian collector--first-rate collection of primitives--by that, we mean stamps printed by local artists in remote parts of the world over a century ago. Very valuable."

"Is he part of this crooked group?"

"Oh, I can't say," Aragon looked uneasy. "I really don't know."

I changed the subject, sensing his sudden unease. "So you're looking at collections today? You buy and sell? or do you act as a middleman?"

"Little of both," Aragon was distracted by his food which was set in front of him.

"You do act for others then?"

"All stamp dealers do," Aragon said between swallows. "We live on commissions sometimes."

"For instance," I sat back, "what would be your commission on the Inverted Jenny?"

Aragon went on eating and eventually replied without looking up, " I have no idea, really no idea."

"You see, Frank," I said confidentially, "I'm trying to find a motive for the theft of the Inverted Jenny. I think whoever stole the stamp from New was given a commission based on its market value by whoever hired him to steal it."

"Sounds reasonable. Very good thinking," Aragon nodded enthusiastically.

"Since murder was involved, I should think that that commission would be quite high, wouldn't you?"

"No idea," Aragon spoke through a mouthful. But I sensed he was evading a discussion. I dropped the subject.

We ate in silence for awhile. We talked about a few trivial matters, then I got the name of Aragon's hotel in case I needed to get in touch with him. Aragon was staying over for only one night. We finished the meal in a discussion on rare books, about which Aragon was well-informed, as they were his hobby.

When I got back to my office, I called Winslow Margin at the stamp shop to see if he had anything to tell me.

"I have the information you want, Mr. Mack. I spoke with the organization in Brussels this morning. It was no problem."

"Okay," I said, "who owns the 1869 Inverted Center?"

"Kyren Vanderlyne."

I did a double-take. "Can we reach him?"

"Yes, through the organization. The secretary will forward any messages to him."

Vanderlyne had the perfect front. "One more question, Winslow. Do you know Hippolyte de Leon?"

"Oh, yes, knowledgeable writer on stamps. But I don't know his real name, if that's what you're looking for."

I called Continental Insurance and asked for John Macdonald. "It's Rudyard Mack," I said when I heard the familiar, rough-edged voice of Storey. "There's a stamp dealer who knows more about the Inverted Jenny than we do. Will you tail him?" I gave him Aragon's name and hotel. "Be careful with him. He's our only lead so far."

Macdonald sounded more responsible than Storey. The organized criminal seemed to change personalities when he became a business executive.

I went upstairs to the main reading rooms and looked through the indices to periodical articles under the subject heading "postage stamps."

There was one article by de Leon in the past year. I wrote out a request slip for the latest volume of the *International Stamp News* and waited for my indicator number to be flashed.

"Hello, Mr. Mack!"

I turned to see Homer Margin standing expectantly behind his spectacles.

Homer stepped close. "Mr. Mack, I've got interesting news about Edgar Berney," he rounded his eyes. "He's offering stamps for sale to members of the staff. It's all very hush-hush."

"He's in the hospital," I said. "How can he sell his stamps from there?"

"He wrote to one of his friends. I'll try to get a copy of the letter if I can."

"No," I said. "Just let me know to whom he sells them."

Homer excitedly stepped away to do what he did best--spying on staff members.

I claimed my periodical. The article by Hippolyte de Leon was easy to find: "Rare Air Mail Stamps." I concentrated on one paragraph:

One of the most prized of the American Air Mails is that elusive Inverted Jenny, a good example of which has been on public display for a quarter of a century in the Miller Collection at the New York Public Library. Although there are 100 of these stamps extant, none has been owned by European collectors. This is a pity as one of these stamps added to any of the airmail collections I have noted above would greatly increase the value of the whole collection.

In collections listed above I noted with a start the name of K. Vanderlyne. I wondered why Frank Aragon only mentioned Vanderlyne's interest in Primitives when he was known to have one of the four important European collections of air mails? Whatever the reason, it now seemed that both James New and Kyren Vanderlyne had been behind the theft of the Library's stamps: New got the Inverted Jenny whereas Vanderlyne got the 1869 Inverted Centers and the 1909 Star Plates. New was dead and Vanderlyne was in Europe hiding behind a legitimate stamp organization. Meanwhile, where had the Inverted Jenny gone?

It was all too pat. By shifting the blame to Europe, the many puzzles about the American participants in the theft remained unanswered. If one supposed that Vanderlyne had New murdered, why did he arrange for an album of New's stamps to be left with Winslow Margin? And who was this Hippolyte de Leon who had taken such a keen interest in the case that he was implicating Edgar Berney in order to divert the investigation? In other words, who was working for whom? And why, oh God! did I have to untangle this mess within one week?

I went upstairs to the Trustees Room. There was to be a monthly meeting of trustees in the afternoon. I had to go over the room carefully for any devices, explosive or otherwise. Since the Library began depending on government grants, its private character and the trustee's practice of meeting in secret were challenged. State legislators passed a law opening the trustees' meetings to the public for the first time in eighty years. From the first open meeting, the trustees replaced their beautifully carved wooden chairs and great oak table with an ordinary long table and folding chairs. Union demonstrators, picketing on the Library's front steps like George Washington's rag-tail army in the early days, marched in, around, and out of the Trustees Room. President Stavoris locked the door after them. He used the incident as an excuse to lock the doors in future when meetings began. For those of the public who attended meetings on time, the trustees dealt only with general issues, whereas financial and controversial subjects were reserved for sub-committees which still met in private. So much for the law!

Still, I was glad for security reasons that the door was shut after the meeting began. Aside from the very rich, the trustees comprised the top people in all the various fields: communications, publishing, manufacturing, oil industry, the church, education, tourism--even some scholars of note. Some of them began taking their places at the table and sorting through pages. Two or three public spectators took seats reserved for them around the sides of the room. I saw Henry Betterton and a tall, fully-proportioned woman come into the room through a hall leading from the executive offices. The woman was listening intently to Betterton who nodded at me. With a broad smile, she broke away and strode toward me.

"Rudy Mack!" she said extending her arm. "Henry has been telling me exciting things about you!"

72

I clasped her hand and felt I was in the presence of a unique and demanding personality.

"I'm Henry's wife," she said. "Don't look so astonished!"

"Oh! Mrs. Betterton." I sensed her full round breasts and slim loins.

"Call me Sybil," she smiled. "We're all in the family. Henry has told me of your determination to find the stamps. I just love detective work. We must talk about it. Come sit over here with me." She led me to the high-backed chairs along one wall. "These meetings must bore you. I'm only here because Henry and I must attend a party directly afterwards."

"It's one of my more pleasurable duties," I said wryly.

She laughed. "I like you, Rudy. We must get to know one another. I know, why don't you come to dinner tomorrow, will you?"

I concealed my surprise. "Very nice," I said. "Thank you."

"Come with Henry, about 6.30. I hope you like lamb chops."

There was a hint of something rather intimate in that last phrase, as if she were implying that I should like her.

I could only nod appreciatively as Stavoris was calling the meeting to order in a loud voice. The director of the American Broadcasting Corporation hurried into the room, was stopped by the Cardinal who whispered in his ear, and continued to his seat with an expression of pleasure and embarrassment at being singled out by the Cardinal for special attention.

Amos Anders gave a brief report in a deferential, self-effacing tone. The subject of the stolen stamps came up. Betterton suggested that they would have to write them off as permanently lost, but said that he would not make a recommendation until the next meeting. Sharply reminded that time was running out, I made my departure from Sybil Betterton. Among the public faces listening to the meeting was Arbuthnott sitting near the door. We exchanged glances discreetly.

My secretary gave me a telephone message from Detective Buckle. When I read it, I reacted as if I had been struck. The fingerprints on New's stamp album which I had asked Buckle to identify belonged to a Kyren Vanderlyne! Vanderlyne must have been in New York and perhaps still was! Now that the mysterious **Vanderlyne** had been definitely linked to James New, I was sure the smart little stamp dealer from Buffalo knew more about him than he told me. I called Frank Aragon's hotel. There was no answer from his room. It was late afternoon. I wished I had not told Macdonald about Aragon. Suddenly, the dandified stamp dealer had become extremely important.

SEVENTEEN

I called Aragon's room on the house phone as soon as I entered his hotel. Still no reply. I went to the lobby to wait and was amused to see the redhead sitting there and reading *Time* magazine.

"Macdonald, or is it Storey this time?" I said.

"Macdonald to you until further notice," he said coldly.

I sat beside him. "Where's Aragon?"

"He gave us the slip, damn him!" Storey looked angry. "But we found out that he's a wheeler-dealer. He must a' met a half dozen guys one after the other in the Plaza coffee shop. I recognized two from the Bonnano family."

"Not your type," I said sarcastically.

"Bastards! I'd drill them for half a buck. Anyway, I'm waiting for Aragon to show up, and we can have a few words. But now you're here, maybe we can wait in his room in more comfort."

"How do I make the difference?" I asked.

"You got a detective I.D. in case we're stopped." Storey stood up. "Come on."

I followed him to the elevators. "We'll look in his room," I said, "but we're not staying."

We took an elevator to the tenth floor and found Aragon's room; Storey took two thin strands of wire from a small leather case, fitted them into the lock, and opened the door. The room had been made up. Not even a scrap of paper was visible. Storey began opening bureau drawers.

"Don't waste your time," I said. I looked round the room as Storey watched me. Then I walked to the bed, shoved my arm between the double mattress and brought out a thin red leather case. "It has an anagram on the front, J.N.," I said. "Looks like we found another part of James New's collection."

"Lemme see," Storey grabbed it from me and began leafing through the pages.

"You won't find the Inverted Jenny there," I warned him.

"I'm not finding much here. There's whole pages that are blank."

"Now you know what he was doing in the Plaza coffee shop. He's been doing business." I began looking in other areas of the room. I opened the closet and took down Aragon's suitcase. "We'd be smart not to let him know that we know." I came across a baggage claim ticket for Grand Central Station in a side pocket of the case. I put it into my coat pocket. "Wait for him downstairs and follow him when he goes out tonight," I instructed Storey, who did not see me pocket the claim ticket. "That's when he'll make the big score."

"Looks like I'm doing your job," Storey complained. "I'm not a detective."

I was apprehensive about staying longer. I took the stamp album from Storey and fitted it back between the mattresses. "Let's go, Macdonald."

We closed the door and walked quickly to the elevators. As we got on the down elevator, the up elevator opened. I glimpsed Frank Aragon getting off before the door of my elevator closed. "Just saw him," I said to Storey. "So you'll just have time for a quick bite before he reappears for his evening jaunt."

"Very funny," Storey said. His florid face took on a sullen cast.

I took a taxi to Grand Central and noted the fare in my expense book. My expenses were looking formidable. Handing Aragon's claim ticket to the baggage clerk, I received a black attaché case in return, took the Lexington Avenue subway downtown, and controlled my curiosity about its contents until I reached the privacy of my apartment.

The case, I discovered, contained hundreds of stamps in plastic envelopes, an automatic pistol, and a letter addressed to Frank Aragon and postmarked a week ago in Buffalo.

I read the letter with difficulty as the handwriting was rushed.

Frank---
When you make contact, remind him to batten down the hatches.--
Vanderlyne

"Batten down the hatches," I said. "Language of a sailor."
The gun was loaded. I unloaded it. I studied the stamps. Some of them had interesting watermarks--otherwise I could only guess that they were rare. None was from the Library's collection. No clues there. My only hope was that Storey alias Macdonald could follow Aragon to his contact and not be seen. I was cooking my dinner when the telephone rang.

Homer Margin reported his findings. "The latest is," he said excitedly, "that Mr. Bugofsky is buying Edgar Berney's stamps!"

I laughed. "That doesn't sound reasonable. Bugofsky doesn't collect stamps. I don't think he even puts them on letters. He told me they don't taste right."

" I couldn't believe it too," Homer cried, "but, by George, you know a friend of Berney told me he delivered a box of stamps to Bugofsky's office."

"Where's Berney?"

"He's resting at home, I hear. He can't walk about yet, I'm told."

"Okay, good work, Homer, keep in touch." I returned to my cooking in time to keep my pork chop from smoking.

When I finished eating, I locked Aragon's stamps, gun, ammunition, letter, and case as separate items into a deep drawer in my small darkroom where I had put New's stamp album. I figured I had a million dollar investment stacked away. Someday someone was bound to come prowling around for it.

I took the subway to Edgar Berney's house and reflected on the possibilities presented by the case so far. The colorful graffiti scrawled all over the subway cars mirrored the ugly jungle of confusion in my mind. Would there be another murder? I had the feeling that my perseverance in the case was going to force another shooting. It was as if the principals in tying themselves into knots to escape detection had to strike out to relieve their frustrations.

The voice of Berney senior challenged me through the apartment door. I watched the eye hole open and listened to the door locks click and slide open in succession.

"You again!" Berney senior said in disgust. He shook his head so that his white goatee seemed to swish in the air.

"Want to see how our patient is," I said stepping into the apartment. I found the lanky figure propped up in bed surrounded by books lying open page down.

"You look ready to go back to work," I said.

Berney smiled wanly. "Mind's willing but the flesh ain't."

"When do you expect to be on your feet?" I asked sitting on the only chair.

"Soon as he's free of suspicion," Berney senior said from the doorway.

"Heh, heh," Berney laughed with embarrassment. "Yo...yo...you don't suspect m... meh...me, do ya?"

"I suspect everyone," I said. "If I didn't, I'd never find the stamps."

75

Berney senior shrugged and shuffled off to the living room.

"Heard from Storey since he visited you as Macdonald in the hospital?" I asked.

"Di...di...did my Dad tell yo...yo...you that?" Berney frowned.

"What was the arrangement between you two? Just the theft of the encyclopedia?"

"Yep," Berney nodded.

"Who's Hippolyte de Leon?"

Berney shrugged and looked concerned, his long face a study of sadness. "Somebody who hates me."

"What stamps are you selling, Edgar?"

Berney picked up his head in surprise. "The...they're mine. I need the mo... money. 'Course I kept my best ones. I'm no fool."

"Why do you need the money? Isn't disability paying enough?"

"Nope, it ain't," Berney said. "Not for me and Dad."

"Did you know they were bought by the Business Manager?"

"Yeah, he con...con...contacted me when he learned that the...the...they were for sale."

"Do you know a stamp dealer in Buffalo named Frank Aragon?"

"Nope," Berney shook his head vigorously. "I seen his catalog, but I don't know him."

I sensed that Berney was telling only half the truth; it was in his nature to conceal some things for his own protection.

"Look, Edgar, that encyclopedia you stole--did you know it was for James New in Buffalo?"

Berney looked up slyly. "Yes, I knew."

"Well then, for God's sake, tell me what the set up was all about. I don't want to drag it out of you."

"Not much to say. All I know is Sto...Storey was to pay me to de...deliver to him. Who murdered New? Your gu. . . gu . . . guess is as go . . . go . . . good as mi . . . mi . . .mine."

I thought Berney's speech was like a lie detector; the more he lied, the more he stuttered.

I got up. "If you think of anything you should be telling me . . . " I stepped quickly into the hall and found Berney senior standing there and listening, "you call me. Don' t forget you owe me for keeping quiet about that encyclopedia."

"Okey-dokey," Berney smiled.

I let myself out and listened to Berney senior throw the locks as I continued to the doorway. A transaction was taking place in the vestibule-- three menacing faces, their black eyes starting with anger as they watched me pass by. In the street, a pimp was beating up his woman whose cries sounded soulless in the bleak darkness. I thought of calling Arbuthnott, just to keep in touch, but decided against it. I didn't try to explain why; I felt that my reluctance had something to do with maintaining my bachelor status.

My instinct led me to Dimeland. The name had been adopted in a much earlier era when dances were actually a dime a time. Not that I planned to dance. I

76

was looking for Sharkey Bugofsky who, on those nights when he was sober enough to walk, frequented the place. Or, so I was told by some of the readers in the Library who patronized it.

The ballroom was crowded. Lennie Allen's orchestra blared a tune that was popular thirty years before. I skirted the tables. A man of a hale and hearty disposition, who read the financial services in the Library, grabbed my arm as if he were going to take me to the dance floor.

"Watchya doin' here? I didn't know you like dancing!" he said.

"I'm working," I said. "Looking for the boss."

"Oh yeah! He's over there!" He pointed to a distant table beyond a crowd of people. There sat Bugofsky and two young women. Bugofsky was refilling the glasses of the women with red wine.

"You know," said the reader of the financial services as I stepped away, "I never seen him dance."

I stood behind the fourth chair at the table. "Anyone sitting here?"

Bugofsky looked up with a beatific smile. "Why, Rudy, nice to see you. Sit down." He introduced me to the ladies. "This is a room full of nostalgia for me," he said waving his arm in a half-circle. "I had my first dates out on that floor--met my first wife there."

The girls giggled shortly.

"No kidding," Bugofsky continued, smiling with a straight mouth, not his usual shark-like grin. "What you drinking, Rudy?"

"Beer," I said.

"The working man's drink for a real hard worker," Bugofsky said to the girls. "You want to dance with one of my ladies?" he asked me.

"Not right away!" I smiled at the girls. "I wanted to talk to you."

Bugofsky called the waiter and signaled what he wanted.

The girls stood up. "See you later, Sharkey baby." They walked away wiggling their behinds.

"They would've given you a free dance," Bugofsky said.

I squirmed uneasily. "The stamps are on my mind."

"Good, good," Bugofsky said pleasantly. "What've you found?"

"That you bought Edgar Berney's stamps."

Bugofsky smiled. "On the orders of Stavoris. So figure that one out."

"Were any of the Library stamps among them?"

"No," Bugofsky snorted. "They weren't worth much."

The waiter deposited a beer and a whisky in front of us.

"Why do you think Stavoris wanted them?" I asked.

"He told me, for his nephew," Bugofsky said taking a gulp of whisky. "But you're making me think, Rudy, and I don't want to think at this time."

"Did Stavoris say anything about Hippolyte de Leon?"

"The commie?" Bugofsky said. "Not after he asked me to find out who he was? Who is he?"

"A pseudonym," I said. "He writes on stamps."

Bugofsky pondered. "You got to go after Stavoris and old Anders. They know more than they're saying."

"How?" I said.

"Go see the guy's nephew, the one with all the stamps. Maybe there's a clue there." Bugofsky called out to a woman passing by.

As she approached I took my leave. Bugofsky took no notice of my departure. He was looking at the woman as if she were his bride.

When I got back into the street, I pondered on the cinema marquees and the brightly lit billboards in Times Square. I thought I should go home and get some sleep, but on a hunch I decided to call in at Frank Aragon's hotel. I found Storey in the lobby.

"I've been chasing a nut case," Storey said. His deep voice had developed a rasp. "Right after you left here, before I could eat, this guy goes charging out of the hotel. I track him over to Grand Central where he's arguing with the baggage claims guy for half an hour. Then he goes to a telephone booth and stays there for almost an hour. Then he comes back to the hotel and stays in his room. So where's the big contact?"

"Sounds like something went wrong," I said. "I'm going up to see him."

"I'm going home," Storey said. "I've had it."

"Say," I stopped him, "why did Stavoris buy Edgar Berney's stamps?"

"I just work for him," Storey smiled and ran his hand through his red locks. "I can't explain him."

Aragon answered the door of his hotel room wearing a dressing-gown over his pajamas, slippers and a pipe in his mouth. Even in this outfit he had the air of a dandy.

"Rudyard Mack!" he exclaimed. "Come in! I've been trying to reach you! This is a stroke of providence."

I found that Aragon was studying stamps under the hotel bed lamp. The red case that he had kept between the mattresses was lying on the bureau and stamps were strewn beside it.

"Sit down, please," he pointed to the chair and perched on the bed. "What brings you here?"

"Passing by," I said.

"Well, I need a detective!" Aragon clasped his hands together. "I've lost some valuable stamps which I checked at Grand Central Station. The clerk gave them to someone else."

"Did you call the police?" I asked innocently.

Aragon made a face. "They can't help. I need you to help me out of the jam I'm in. You see, I had a client who was prepared to purchase them for a lot of money."

"Who's he?" I asked casually. Although I felt fortunate to have got my hands on his stamps, I did feel sorry for him. He was distraught.

Aragon shook his head. "I have to keep the names of my clients a secret for their own protection. I hope you understand." His thin features adopted a closed, secretive look.

I tried another tack. "Who do you suspect?"

"It could have been anyone who found the claims ticket."

"Any rivals in business?" I asked.

"Yes, but I can't see them stealing my stamps. Not even Winslow Margin would do it!"

78

"You didn't steal the stamps in the first place?" I asked suggestively. Aragon looked startled. I continued, "You didn't steal them from James New?"

Aragon was thunderstruck.

"Don't answer in case you incriminate yourself," I said. "However, if I'm going to help you I would like the truth."

"You seem to know more about me than you let on," Aragon said softly.

"Maybe," I looked hard at him, "but that's not an answer."

"Well," Aragon smiled apologetically, "I'm handling them for someone who stole them from James New."

"And if you lose them?"

"I lose my life."

"So, Frank, we can come to terms, right?"

"Give me time," he pleaded. "I'm staying on a couple of days to find the stamps. If we find them, I'll tell you who I'm working for. It'll help your case, Rudyard, even lead you to the Inverted Jenny, I think."

"It's a deal," I said. "I'll look for 'em. Meanwhile you stay out of trouble."

I left the hotel with a sense of cautious jubilation. I wondered how soon I should return the stamps. I couldn't do it too soon; it would look fishy to Aragon. But then, I had only a few days to solve the case. Aragon was the key to opening the locks on the door leading to a solution.

I went back to my office to put in an hour of paperwork and found a special delivery letter from Switzerland which I opened with anticipation. Neatly typed, the letter was signed, "Yours fraternally, Peter Zins."

Dear Detective Mack,

As I promised when we spoke in recent days I give you information on how to watch for your stamps.

You were right to contact Zurich. Today the Germans are the best stamp counterfeiters and many work in this city. Since this kind of police work is unknown to you, I shall explain from the beginning.

(1) The easiest counterfeiting is to reperforate a stamp with a perforating machine. This would be done in the case of the 1869 inverted centers because they are rare enough for the average dealer to be unaware of reperforation. It is more certain to be done with the Inverted Jenny because there are only 100 of them. A danger is that a dealer could have the stamp's perforations verified by your American Philatelic Society. Most are not so scrupulous, however.

(2) Rebuilding a mutilated stamp by melding new paper into the main body and continuing the design is a common disguise but difficult artistically. You can discover these stamps by dipping the "suspects" into the proper solution or measuring their thickness with a micrometer. Common stamps can be increased in value and disguised by adding a curlicue to the design. This fools many collectors. 30 to 40% of stamps we examine fall into this latter category.

How to catch the sale of stolen stamps

We study the auction catalogs. Stamps above a certain value are reproduced in them and we can study the perforations. Stolen stamps are inserted in legitimate collections and auctioned as if they always belonged to those collections. In these cases provenances can be made up quickly and go unchecked because of the great number of stamps being auctioned.

Then stamps easy to recognize are sold to private collectors who show their collections only to close friends. You may know the case of your Mr. Eli Lilly, the owner of your big drug manufacturing who collected the world's most valuable stamps in a small room in his offices. No one knew of this collection until he died a score of years ago. His collection could not be duplicated today because no one person is rich enough to buy all those precious stamps. You will find your Inverted Jenny in such a collection, I think.

Legitimate stamp organizations can be used as a "front" for getting rid of "hot" stamps to unsuspecting purchasers.

Transport

Rare stamps will not be sent by ordinary mail for fear of loss. If sent by registered mail with a value about $50,000, customs will want to see the parcel. Moreover, I am sorry to admit that registered mail is no longer guaranteed of delivery in Europe. Thefts by postal people are endemic here. I believe only Los Angeles and Chicago in your country suffer from the same high rate of larceny. Your stamp thieves will pay the round trip air fare to bring the stamps to Europe. When the stamps are doctored and if they will find higher prices in America, such as early American stamps which can fill gaps in Americana collections, the same courier returns with them to America.

We have found that organized crime families have been used as couriers in recent years because they have established patterns of communication and know state officials who can help them if something goes wrong. Also, they have experience in carrying large amounts of cash, and have means of laundering money.

Buyers

As for naming American buyers of stamps who deal with the Corporation Internationale des Negociants en Timbre Postes, I am told by my superior that it is against our rules to give names of possible suspects. If you were connected with Interpol it might be different. I am sure you understand. I can assure you within reason, however, that the stamps have not gone through Zurich.

But there are more than five million serious stamp collectors in your country, any one of whom could have the stamps. You must advertise the theft widely. For instance, *Linn's Stamp News* has 80,000 subscribers and your various stamp associations have memberships in the tens of thousands. A stamp collector reads anything and everything he can about stamps. So, my dear Mack, you must advertise, as you Americans say, and sit back to wait for the dividends to come in.

I can hazard you will find the most valuable stamps in one or two big collections (here I mean the 1867 30-cent Franklin and the 4-cent bluish Washington). The minor stamps, such as the imperforate Crawford set of 1875 reprints or the 1857-60 stamps, the Lincoln 2-cent blues and the 5-cent 1847s, will be scattered to the four winds and may not surface for decades.

Good hunting!

EIGHTEEN

I spent the next day on Library routine--patrolling the corridors and the reading rooms--until it was six and the time to meet Henry Betterton at the Fifth Avenue entrance. Only one personal note jarred the day. Arbuthnott called and wanted to see me that evening. She was upset when I told her I was having drinks at the Betterton's.

"They'll co-opt you, those bastards, and you'll be just as corrupt as they are," she warned. "Come back to me, Rudy."

I could think of no reason for the Bettertons to invite me to their home, especially as I was not of their social level, as it were. Yet I had always sensed Henry Betterton's friendly interest in me, and I was intrigued by the apparent sexual overture issued by Sybil Betterton, although I knew its danger. She was a tall, dark-haired beauty with long shapely legs and a full sensuous figure. I would have been a fool to resist.

Betterton was five minutes late. He ran down the marble stairway and swung a briefcase like a boy let out of school.

"Hope you had a hard day, Rudyard," Betterton called over his shoulder as he pushed on the circular doors, "because you'll appreciate my wife's cooking all the more. As for me, I need a drink."

I ran after him down the steps to a black limousine at the Fifth Avenue curb. A uniformed chauffeur opened the back door for us.

"These non-profit institutions are like leaky boats. You got to keep bailing and put out more sail all the time." Betterton sat in first, and, as I sat beside him, he pulled open a drawer in the back of the seat in front of us and revealed a miniature bar. "How about a scotch? soda?"

"Yes, please," I said responding to his enthusiasm.

The car started up and smoothly sped away. Betterton quickly poured the drinks, handed me a glass, clinked it with his, and took a deep swallow. Betterton pried off his shoes and stretched back in the seat.

"Did the trustees have a meeting?" I asked.

"Our Committee on Finances did," Betterton said. "We discussed a subject that would interest you: the stamp theft. Since Detective Buckle officially informed me that the Manhattan Police Department considered the case a dead letter, I proposed that we accept payment from Continental Insurance and shelve the issue."

"But I was told nothing would be done until the end of the week," I said.

"Don't worry, Rudyard," Betterton laughed. "Mr. Stavoris argued on your behalf. I just have the committee's permission to settle the issue at the end of the week. How on earth are you going to catch the thief in a few days when the Police Department has thrown in the towel. But you're the bulldog type, aren't you? Stubborn."

"Well, my thanks to Mr. Stavoris," I said taking a drink.

"Yes. I don't understand his interest in the theft," Betterton shook his head. "He seems to think about it a great deal, as if it were a personal tragedy."

"His nephew collects stamps," I said.

Betterton laughed. "That's not enough involvement to explain his actions. No, he's got a large interest in Continental Insurance, and for some reason, he's loathe to see it pay the bill. Surely the thousands it has to pay won't damage the company. Good heavens, if it's that close to the wall, we'd better look elsewhere for an insurance carrier!"

"Maybe he really does think the stamps will be found," I said.

Betterton eyed me closely. "You think they will be, don't you, Rudyard? Why?"

"I'm following some leads," I said. "There's a guy called Kyren Vanderlyne who's key to the whole business. I just have to find him."

"Vanderlyne? Sounds Dutch? Where does he live?"

"Belgium."

"Oh, I see. Rather difficult to find him by Friday, don't you think?"

"He's in New York, I'm pretty sure," I said. The drink was making me talk more than I wanted. "I know for certain he has the Inverted Jenny."

"What did you say? How can you be certain?" Betterton sat up.

"Oh!" I checked myself as I realized I was talking too much. "It's just a strong hunch, that's all. I'll tell you Friday. It's too soon to be making my report anyway."

Betterton was silent for awhile, then said, "Maybe you need more help. You can't handle it all on your own." Betterton looked concerned.

"Thank you, sir, I'll let you know," I said. "But we could use a new man on the Fifth Avenue entrance, someone who really does check people's bags. I think we're losing too many books that way and it detracts me from the stamp investigation."

We discussed security arrangements until we came to Betterton's residence on the north shore of Long Island. We drove along a lane to the porticoed front. Betterton slipped his shoes on and led me out the car door, which the chauffeur held open, up the steps of the verandah and into a large hallway.

"I think we'll find her over here," he said.

I followed him through a sitting room out onto a patio at the side of the house. Sybil Betterton was reclining on a chaise-longue. She had pulled her skirt up to her thighs displaying her shapely legs to the sun. My interest quickened. I took her hand with as much composure as I could muster.

"How good to see you!" Sybil said with emphasis. "I suppose Henry has already offered you a drink?"

"Will the same suit you?" Betterton asked as he stepped to a sideboard.

"All right," I said and sat on the chair beside Sybil which she pointed to. "But not strong, please."

Sybil and I regarded one another for a moment. I liked the intelligence in Sybil's strong face. Boldness in women usually turned me away, but with Sybil, her self-possession was combined with a sensuousness that both attracted and intrigued me.

"Have another gin, dear?" Betterton asked.

"Yes, dear," Sybil said, staring with an impish smile at me. "I'm game for anything tonight."

I smiled. Betterton seemed to be consciously ignoring our flirtation. The sun balanced on the rim of the horizon behind us.

"Isn't it peaceful here?" Sybil sighed. "In our early married life, we lived in Manhattan and thought it was heaven. Now we think it's hell."

"You must learn to avert your eyes, ignore the ugliness," I volunteered.

"Thank you, sir." I took my scotch and soda from Betterton.

"Don't be so formal!" Sybil protested. "His name is Henry. And I'm Sybil. Come now, Rudyard, relax, you're with friends," she smiled dazzlingly.

"Right!" Betterton said with a tone of reserve indicating he would not like me to address him as Henry in front of the management and trustees.

"Just force of habit," I explained. "I'll find it easy to call you Sybil."

The house bell rang shrilly from inside the house.

"The guests are beginning to arrive," Sybil got to her feet. "Henry, show Rudyard the conveniences." She disappeared into the house.

"Bottom's up," Betterton said, raising his glass and draining it with one long swallow.

"Are you having a party?" I asked, alarmed at being expected to mix with their class of people.

"Just a few friends," Betterton explained. "Buffet style--nothing elaborate. Come on, Rudy, I'll show you where you can wash your hands and, uh, by the way, where you can leave your gun and holster of which I just caught a glimpse a moment ago."

"Sorry," I said following him into the house and up the stairs. From the upstairs windows I noticed the sun had disappeared.

The party took place in the large back sitting room. Several couples were sitting, some standing, while they chatted and drank. Sybil took me by the hand and introduced me to two women, neither of whom was attractive. They talked continuously, thus giving me the opportunity to survey the guests while I pretended to listen. I saw President William Stavoris enter with his bird-like wife. She was petite, her nose was like a beak and she twittered when she spoke. At the buffet table I found myself alone with Stavoris.

"Mr. Betterton told me you kept the committee from closing the case. Thanks, sir," I said.

Stavoris looked round with some surprise, his bushy eyebrows raised in question, his hard eyes piercing. "I want to say the same to you, when you get the stamps back, of course. Don't disappoint me."

"I think I need an explanation from you," I said carefully. "Frankly, I can't figure your involvement in the case. I'm referring to your telephone conversations with Winslow Margin about the stolen stamps. You know, of course, that it was not Margin with whom you spoke but with an impostor."

Stavoris paused, holding a forkful of potato salad, and stared at me in disbelief. "I could have sworn it was Margin." He frowned quizzically as if he thought that I was misleading him.

"Then there was your purchase of Edgar Berney's stamps without notifying me."

"Well," Stavoris growled, "we were warned by Hippolyte de Leon that Berney had the stolen stamps. I thought I'd buy them to be on the safe side. Besides, they made a nice gift for my nephew."

"I'd like to meet your nephew," I said firmly.

"You can when he gets home for vacation. He's in school in Brussels."

"Brussels!" I frowned. "Why there?"

Stavoris looked faintly amused. "He's learning French in a school there. Is it important?"

"It may be just a coincidence, but that's the center for international stamp theft," I informed him, giving him a hard stare.

Stavoris laughed abruptly. "Well, my nephew's a good boy and collects only his own stamps."

Perceiving that Stavoris's affable armor had no weak points, I changed my tactics and determined on a frontal thrust. "Your friend, John Macdonald of Continental Insurance, was the man who stole the stamps from the Library."

Stavoris's heavy cheeks collapsed. He stared at me in anger. "How do you know that?"

"He's as good as admitted it to me," I said. "And he fits the description."

Stavoris smiled stiffly. "You've got the wrong man, Rudy. I've known and dealt with John for many years. I've had a lot of trust in him. Now, I don't want to hear any more nonsense about him."

Stavoris turned away abruptly just when Betterton suddenly appeared in front of me.

"Don't talk shop," Betterton said between his teeth. "Forget you're a goddamn detective for once." He waved me away to the side. "Eat your food." He stepped away to other guests.

Chastened, I was left to my thoughts. Stavoris was either a fool or he was lying. If he was lying, then it was possible that he had the stolen stamps. It was possible that he had used James New as a red herring to divert the police. It was possible that he had employed Kyren Vanderlyne to murder New. But why did he want to keep the case open? I was roused from my reverie by Betteron playing the piano. After a few popular songs, Betterton played Mozart's "Eine Kleine Nacht Music." Someone asked him for Chopin, and he obliged. His talent made the evening enjoyable.

As the guests departed, I felt uncomfortable remaining behind, but Sybil smiled at me as if I were the family confidante. When the last couple had gone, I expected Betterton to drive me to the train, but Betterton disappeared upstairs. I was left alone with Sybil.

"Have coffee with me?" she suggested as she poured two cups. She brushed her long dark hair back over her shoulders as if she were preparing to relax.

"Fine, but I should be going."

"Don't be silly," she said. "You'll sleep here tonight and drive in with Henry in the morning." She brought the coffee and, as we sipped it, she took me round the room to show me the objets d'art and the paintings. When she stood directly in front of me as we looked at some red abstract, I could no longer refuse the invitation. I came against her and clasped her breast with one hand while I put down my cup and put down her cup. I turned her round and we kissed long and excitably. I put my hand under her skirt and slipped it up to her panties which I pulled down. I felt the round firm cheeks of her behind and moved my hand gently against the warm and hairy crotch.

"Let's go to my room," she said, "where we can be more comfortable."

I was delighted by her body and the calm, aggressive way she made love. I lay with her in my arms before I fell asleep. My last thought was to marvel that Henry Betterton had given me such a treat. I didn't see that I deserved it in any way.

NINETEEN

I made love to Sybil in the morning and came down to breakfast to find Betterton waiting for me.

"I've eaten breakfast," Betterton said impatiently, "and since I have a heavy day before me would you mind a simple meal? I don't like to hurry you."

"Not at all," I said pleasantly. I swallowed the juice and then the hot coffee which Betterton set in front of me. Putting a breakfast roll in my pocket and strapping on my gun and holster which he left on the side table for me, I stood ready to go.

Betterton looked pleased. "I suppose you've said good-bye to Sybil." He led the way to the car in the front drive, patted the chauffeur on the shoulder, and stretched out in the back seat.

I sat stiffly beside him and wondered if he would inquire whether I had slept comfortably. But Betterton chatted about the guests at the party until the chauffeur, stopping the car at the first news vendors, handed us the *New York Times* and the *Wall Street Journal*. Betterton began reading the *Journal* intently. I read the *Times* and munched my breakfast roll. About the time we reached Manhattan, I discovered a small item in the second section entitled: "Insurance Executive Murdered." I glanced over the first lines with mild curiosity. Apparently yesterday evening, the police had discovered the body stuffed into the wall of a deserted building on the Lower East Side. The man was dead only a few hours and tentatively identified as John Macdonald with Continental Insurance. I gripped the paper and reread the lines. The victim may have been trafficking in drugs, according to the police. I knew better: the victim had been trafficking in stamps. I tried to keep my composure and said nothing to Betterton.

"Here we are," Betterton said suddenly. "I'm dropping you off just three blocks from the Library, Rudyard. I have to get to my real business."

"Thanks, Henry," I said stepping out. "I really enjoyed the evening."

Betterton waved and the black limousine moved away into the uptown traffic.

I was a little shaken. The first question was who murdered John Macdonald alias Storey? Was it the same group that murdered James New? Was he a victim of infighting in his own group? Probably the former. And if so, might I be the next victim? After all, if Storey had been stupid enough to be seen trailing Frank

Aragon, the boys behind Aragon must have thought that he had stolen Aragon's case of stamps. I wondered if Storey had told them that I was working with him.

My secretary said that Bugofsky wanted to see me immediately.

Sharkey Bugofsky was in a foul mood. His office smelt of Scotch whisky. "Last night a woman was almost raped in the third floor washroom," he shouted. "Where the hell were you?"

"What time was that?" I asked.

"Eight o'clock, I think. Says this big guy pushed his way in behind her, and, if she hadn't screamed, there would have been hell to pay."

"She wasn't raped then?"

"Did I say she was raped?" Bugofsky roared. "Listen carefully, I said she was almost raped and would have been raped had our guard not gone to her rescue. Unfortunately, the idiot let the rapist get away."

"Our evening security worked okay then," I said.

"I don't give a..." Bugofsky paused for a noun to enter his head, but when one did not, he swallowed hard. "I've got to meet those feminists from the Allen Room again. An army of them's coming up here in one hour. God, I wish I could crawl into a hole!"

"Tell them we can't work round the clock," I said. "And we can't control minds and the whims of our readers."

"Ah, but Rudy," he said raising an index finger. "They think we can! That's my problem, you see! They think I'm responsible for the mind set of every screwball male reader. Thank God, they haven't yet held me responsible for every female reader!"

"I'd like to help, but I'm devoting myself to the stamp theft," I said with a faint smile.

"If you think this is funny, I'll fire you," Bugofsky warned. "Now, beat it, and get some progress on that goddamn case. I haven't had one memo from you on it."

"I'm getting close," I said as I left the office.

Better to say that the case was drawing close to me, that events were closing in on me. Homer Margin passed me in the hall, stopped, wheeled round and came back with a worried look.

"Didn't see you," he said, "which is remarkable because I've been looking for you. Winslow's in trouble."

I sighed. "He's being followed, I guess."

"That's right," Homer said nervously. "He's afraid to open his store, only goes for important appointments. He's back living with me. Can you do something?"

"Yes, I will," I said. "Tell him I'll call him later."

A faint look of hope came into Homer's stern but saddened face, and he hurried away worriedly. I remarked the change that had come over him since being reunited with Winslow. He was no longer haughty, rather more considerate of others.

My aim was to flush out Kyren Vanderlyne. I walked to the midtown post office and rented a post office box. I took the subway home and, on entering my apartment, went immediately to the stamps. They were still where I had left them. I composed a brief notice: "Found. Packets of rare stamps and red case initialed J.N." I included the Post Box number for respondents and called it in to the *New York Times*. It would appear in tomorrow's issue.

I called Frank Aragon at his hotel.

"I've been waiting to hear from you," Aragon said snappily. "What's up?"

"I want you to identify some stamps," I said. "Will you meet me in an hour at Winslow Margin's store?"

"Winslow Margin, eh?" Aragon clucked. "So he's been in on it all the time."

"We can't be sure. You have to see these stamps."

"You can be sure I'll be on time," Aragon said eagerly.

I hung up and dialed Homer Margin's apartment. "Winslow, who's been following you?"

"Two men, sort of criminal types, I'd say."

"Are they waiting for you now?"

"Just a moment." Winslow came back on the line in a few seconds. "They're parked in the street."

"Look," I said. "Get in a taxi and come to your store right away. I'll be waiting for you."

"You don't think they'll try to attack me?" Winslow asked nervously.

"No, no," I said. "No fear of that."

I added "yet" to myself after he hung up. I took one of the envelopes of stamps that I had found in Aragon's briefcase and put it in my pocket. As I headed for the door, my phone rang. It was Arbuthnott Vine.

"How was the party?"

"Lot of fun." I tried to sound enthusiastic. "But look, sweetheart, I'm in a hurry."

"Did you see in the paper about Macdonald?" Arbie said hurriedly. "Poor Storey finally got what he's been giving others."

"I saw it," I said.

"I'm worried about you, Rudy. Be careful."

"I'm staying away from the Lower East Side," I said. "I'll call you later."

"Let's get together tonight," she suggested.

Fifteen years ago I might have agreed. Today, I didn't feel up to it. "Can't," I said, "I'm on to something hot."

"Do you mean the case or Sybil Betterton?" she asked and slammed down the receiver.

I made a little grimace of contrition and dashed out of the apartment. I arrived outside Margin's store in time to meet Winslow's taxi. Up the street, I saw a car pull over to the curb and two men behind the windshield.

Winslow saw the direction of my gaze. "It's them. What do you think they want?"

"Let's get inside," I said urgently, "and I'll tell you."

As soon as Winslow had fumblingly opened the door, I informed him of my plan to offer Frank Aragon the packet of stamps I had in my pocket. I warned him that they belonged to the James New collection.

"Here," I said putting the stamps on the front table. "Turn on your big light and start studying them. If Aragon asks where you got them, just say 'from a reputable source.'"

Winslow grinned and began sorting out the stamps as I returned to the street. I took out my gun and checked to see that it was loaded. I replaced it in my holster and walked up the street to the car. The men inside looked to be in their mid-twenties. The window on the curbside was open.

"Hello boys," I said.

They nodded sullenly.

"I understand you want to see Mr. Winslow Margin. I'll take you to him."

"Bugger off."

"Maybe you'd better bugger off," I said. "Mr. Margin is getting tired of seeing you."

"Who are you?" one of the men demanded.

"I'm looking into the murder of John Macdonald."

The young men blanched.

"I think you know all about it," I continued. "But what you don't know is that his real name was Storey, and he was a member of a New Jersey crime family."

"We don't know what you talking about."

"You'll find out soon enough," I smiled and moved to the rear of the car. I took out my notebook and jotted down the license number, the make and color of the car, and descriptions of the two men.

The man on the passenger side got out and with a fierce look approached me. Able to gauge his height, I added 5 feet 10 inches in my description.

"What are yer doin'?" he demanded nervously.

"Some New Jersey relatives would like to know about you two," I said, putting my book away.

"Look, mister, we don't want to make trouble. You got us mixed up with somebody else. We know nothing about murder or this guy you think we're tailin'."

At that moment a taxi turned into the street, and I saw Aragon staring in surprise at me from the back seat. The taxi screeched to a stop, and Aragon jumped out. I observed the surprise and then alarm spread over the young thug's face.

"Rudy, what's happening?" Aragon cried.

"We're having a mild confrontation," I said.

"Okay!" the thug said. "We'll take a hint and move off." He jumped into his car which started up immediately and followed the taxi down the street. I had a fleeting suspicion that they knew Aragon.

"Who were they?" Aragon asked.

"I'm trying to find someone who can tell me," I said. "Come on, Margin is in his store."

"I haven't seen him for a long time," Aragon said. "Never wanted to deal with him because he's such a crook."

"Naturally," I nodded.

We climbed the stairs, and I held open the door to Margin's store which Aragon proudly passed through as if he were on an inspection tour.

"Winslow Margin! You old rascal! There you are!" Aragon cried, stepping quickly to Winslow and throwing out his hand.

Winslow had a shy smile and shook Aragon's hand perfunctorily. He was wearing his green eye shade and gray smock and looking very professional.

"Mr. Mack tells me you have stamps that could interest me. How are you, by the way? You don't look any older? Business been good?"

"Business is fair. These are the stamps he saw," Winslow said, displaying the packet taken from Aragon's case.

Aragon's eyes gave a quick look of recognition, but Aragon kept his composure and examined the stamps carefully. He turned to me. "These were stolen from me all right." He studied the stamps again.

"Stolen?" Winslow looked puzzled. "I didn't think they could be because I received them from a reputable source."

"What source?" Aragon demanded.

"Confidential," Winslow said, "but I've always found him honest. In fact, he told me he had bought them from the collection of the late James New."

Aragon suddenly lost his composure. His face went white. His forehead glistened with perspiration.

"How could they have been yours?" Winslow said matter-of-factly.

"I might have been mistaken," Aragon swallowed. He paused and then sputtered nervously, "Could it be arranged for me to meet this client of yours, Winslow?"

"I could ask him," Winslow said with concern. "If I explain the circumstances I think he would meet you. But remember, Frank, he is my customer."

"Come, come, now," Aragon clucked. "Don't you see! He may have the rest of the stamps which were stolen from me! The person who took them probably said they were James New's in order to sell them."

"Reasonable chain of events," I said.

"Oh! Please persuade him to tell me who sold him the stamps." Aragon looked pleadingly at me. His jauntiness had vanished as if the dandy had been transformed into a frightened clerk.

"The only clue we have," I pulled a piece of note paper from my pocket, "is this letter which came with the stamps. Notice it's addressed to 'Frank' and is signed 'Vanderlyne'. You know, that mysterious Vanderlyne I've been trying to find."

Aragon stared at the letter and then looked accusingly at me. "You know where the rest of the stamps are, don't you? You found who took them, didn't you?"

"Don't jump to conclusions, Frank," I put a restraining hand on his shoulder. "Their recovery means a lot to you, I know, but we have to think clearly if we want them back. Now tell me, who is Vanderlyne? Or where is he?"

"I can't tell you that," Aragon said, "no, really I cannot unless," he paused, "you tell me who gave Winslow these stamps."

"Is that reasonable?" I looked at Winslow.

89

"I'll check with my client," Winslow said, touching his fingers to his mustache. "I'm sorry, but it looks like everything depends on his willingness to be identified."

"That's okay!" Aragon smiled, recovering his composure. "I'm sure when he hears how much it will help our detective, he'll be agreeable. Now, I've got to run to an important engagement. Nice seeing you again, Winslow. Guard those stamps with your life. Ring me, Rudyard, eh?"

He disappeared out the door, and we listened to him descend the stairs.

"He's got me," I said looking at the floor. "Even if we do get somebody to pretend to be your client and give Frank a phony name for the guy who supposedly sold the stamps, we can't be sure that Frank will give us the real Vanderlyne. He's just as likely to produce a fraud as we are. No! The only power we hold over him is that he knows we have his stamps, and we know they were stolen from James New. He has to get them back at all cost."

"Then we've got him!" Winslow grabbed up the packet of stamps. "I'll put these in my safe deposit box in the bank."

"Good idea," I nodded. "You're going to be followed. They'll think all the stamps are in there."

"You come with me, then," Winslow looked worried.

"No, it's got to look routine," I said. I picked up the Vanderlyne note which Aragon had left on the table and pocketed it.

"Suppose they kill me?" Winslow asked.

"They'd be more likely to kill me," I corrected him. "I'm going in the opposite direction. Turn off the lights and we'll go down."

As I waited for Winslow Margin to close up his shop, I reflected on the possibility that Aragon no longer trusted me and that Aragon suspected that I had the stolen case and its contents. Of course, the mistake Aragon had made was to have Storey killed without checking into his background. Obviously, he actually believed he had killed an insurance executive, Macdonald, who had been following him around in the hopes of recovering stolen stamps on behalf of the New York Public Library. Or maybe he thought he was another private detective. Poor Storey! I picked up the telephone and dialed the number Storey had given me. A low-toned male voice almost whispered, "yes." I pictured Storey's silent friend always in the driver's seat. I hardened my voice. "You know who killed the redhead?" I gave him the license number and description of the car. "Two dumb guys." I hung up.

Winslow was rattling his keys impatiently.

"Look," I said sharply. "We've got to move fast. Homer can be our mysterious client. When you get home you can explain the deal to him. I'll call Frank and arrange a meeting at a cafe I know on Third Avenue. Eight tonight."

"I don't think Homer's going to be happy," Winslow said.

"Tell him it's very important to the Library," I said. "He'll do it."

TWENTY

I reached Aragon at his hotel and arranged for the meeting that evening. From the unctuous tone of Aragon's voice, I figured Aragon would not come alone. He would have someone in the background. When I called Winslow I asked him to make sure Homer would look like a rich dealer in stamps.

"As soon as he comes home from the Library," Winslow said. "I'll go to work on him."

When I met them at the cafe, Homer was wearing his best suit--a navy-blue pin-stripe--and a white tie with a gold tie-clip. He affected a superior air, rather like his attitude in the Library when speaking with readers.

"Winslow told me the whole story," Homer said nonchalantly, "but what I don't understand is just where are his stamps and other paraphernalia?"

"I have them," I smiled. "Right here in this bag."

"And all we want in return is the identity of one man?" Homer asked.

"Right, Mr...uh...I didn't catch your name," I looked expectantly at both Margins.

"We decided not to give him one," Winslow explained. "If he remains anonymous, no one can check up on him."

"Okay," I agreed. "Look out! Here comes Frank now."

We watched Aragon peer about him at the entrance, then spot our table and wind his way past the intervening tables to us. Homer did not stand up to shake his hand when introduced. He simply motioned with his head for Aragon to sit down as in a B-Western movie.

"Mr. Mack informs me you were robbed." Homer looked concerned. "I've brought the materials that were sold to me for you to identify." He signaled me to open the bag.

"Very kind of you, sir," Aragon said pleasantly. "I'm most indebted to you." He watched me pull out the packets of stamps. "Yes, those are mine." I pulled out the case. "Yes, yes." I pulled out the pistol. "Um hm," Aragon nodded.

"There is, however, one problem," Homer said. "There is reason to believe that these stamps belonged to the late James New. I shall have to have them identified by the New estate trustees."

"I'm agreeable," Aragon cried, examining the stamps. "I'm just so happy to know they've been recovered. I was afraid I'd lost tens of thousands of dollars."

I raised my eyebrows at Winslow. This was not the answer we expected.

"Good," Homer said quickly, "I'll leave them in the care of Detective Mack. When we can prove them to be yours, we can come to an arrangement for their return." He stood up. "Come, Winslow, my good man."

A waitress stepped quickly to the table, but Homer put out his hand as if to ward off an advancement and led Winslow toward the door.

"I'll be in touch," Winslow called to Aragon as they left.

I ordered beers for Aragon and myself.

"He's a mysterious character," Aragon said. "Why won't he give me his name?"

"If you were he, would you give your name in a situation where there is a possibility of a criminal conspiracy?" I asked. "I think he's extraordinary to do as much as he has."

Aragon looked at me as if struggling with doubts. The waitress put our beers on the table.

"Is that all?" she demanded.

When I nodded, she gave me the check.

"How are you going to verify those aren't New's stamps?" Aragon asked suddenly.

"Call the lawyer of the estate, I suppose. Mr. Harriman is his name. But our mysterious friend will look into that."

"I hope it won't take long," Aragon frowned. "I have to sell those stamps and get out of here. You know, these New York hotels cost too much."

I cleared my throat. "You will remember, Frank, that I recovered the stamps for you."

"Yes, yes, Rudy, of course I will. Let's see, I guess I can afford to give you a commission on this sale. How's that?" Aragon asked cheerfully, but I could see that he was still very worried.

"That's fine," I said and finished my beer. "Now if you don't mind accompanying me to my apartment house with this valuable merchandise." I stood up and picked up the bag. "It's just around the corner."

As we walked down the street, I noticed that a car followed us cautiously. By keeping Aragon with me, I was certain they would leave me alone. Aragon, however, seemed quite happy to leave arrangements the way they were--a puzzling situation since I was positive that the stamps had been stolen from New. I said good-bye at the door to Aragon.

"Just a couple of more days, Frank, and then you can quit this ugly, rip-off of a city."

Aragon actually nodded in agreement, as if he were confident that the stamps would soon be returned to him. I put the stamps back in my darkroom and dialed Harriman's number in Buffalo from the card the lawyer had give me. His wife answered, and, after I succeeded in establishing my identity and the urgency of the problem, she told me that Harriman was in New York City--she called it "the Big Apple"--and gave me his telephone number. I got Harriman right away. I explained about the stolen stamps and Aragon's claim to them.

"I'll come right over," Harriman said in a brusque business-like way.

"It's getting late, " I said. "You can come tomorrow."

"No!" Harriman insisted. "If there is even the remotest chance they belong to the New estate, my duty is to look at them as soon as possible. I'm close enough to visit you tonight."

I opened the door to a steady buzzing twenty minutes later and presently the stocky Harriman with the stolid look that I remembered seeing last at New's funeral, came to the door.

"Lucky I was in New York," Harriman said following me to the living room where excitedly he began to examine the stamps I had laid out on the table. He studied each closely with great patience. I watched him in silence for over half an hour.

"It looks as if it is a false alarm," Harriman said getting to his feet and stretching. "None of these stamps belonged to James New."

Astounded, I said nothing.

"I'm sorry to disappoint you," Harriman smiled, "and myself, but the fellow, Aragon, probably does own them."

I was bewildered. I had seen the New album in Aragon's hotel room. It resembled the New album I had found in Winslow Margin's post box. Surely these stamps had been stolen from New.

"Wait, Mr. Harriman," I cried, scooping the stamps back into their packages. "Stay for a drink. I'd like to talk to you about this whole strange business."

"Oh, I'd like to, but I have a busy day laid on for tomorrow. Got to get some rest. We'll talk later, Mr. Mack." Harriman strode rapidly to the door and let himself out. I barely had time to get to the door to see him enter the elevator.

I was positive that Harriman was mistaken. I had been ready to show him the stamps in the New album that I found in Margin's post box, but a sixth sense restrained me.

My phone rang. It was Sybil Betterton. She was lonely. She wanted to meet me tomorrow night. She would take me to dinner. Henry was going to be tied up in business all evening. I readily agreed to meet her. I thought that she was an intriguing woman. In fact, she seemed to be as much a puzzle as the case of the stolen stamps. As I went to bed, I had a fleeting thought of Arbuthnott Vine. I saw her chairing a union committee meeting.

I awakened to a heavy slapping on my shoulder and the glare of a flashlight in my face.

"Get on your feet, you stupid bastard! We ain't got all night."

I rolled out of bed and stood up. I felt the cold muzzle of a gun against my stomach.

"Turn on the light!"

I turned on the wall light and saw that the intruder was a tall, heavy-set man I had not seen before. There was an ugly scar across his face.

"Stamps! Get them!" The thug gave my shoulder a hard push.

As I stepped into the hall, the hall light went on and I saw a smaller man standing with a gun in his hand by the door of the apartment. I went to the dark room and retrieved the stamps in the case belonging to Aragon. The thug grabbed the case from me, opened it, and looked through it. He knew exactly what he wanted. He touched the pistol and counted the packets of stamps.

"They'd better be all here, fella," the thug said.

My stomach felt like cold mash. Would they kill me now?

"Put a coat on," the big man ordered.

I took a raincoat from the hall closet and put it on over my pajamas. "I want shoes," I said.

"Hurry up!" the thug waved his gun.

I found my shoes under my bed with my socks stuffed in them. I put my socks and shoes on while the big man stood over me breathing heavily.

"Where are we going?" I asked.

"Surprise."

When we reached the man at the door, I recognized the thug who had come out of the car to challenge me that afternoon by Winslow Margin's stamp shop. He gave me a snarl of recognition.

It was remarkably easy for them to escort me by the doorman. They both smiled affably at my sullen look as if I were unable to appreciate a good joke. They took me to their car, double-parked, with a third man at the wheel. I got into the back with the big thug, and we sped away to the west side. I had a sense of deja vu. Could I be lucky twice in a row? Very unlikely. When I tried to ask a question, the big man told me to shut up. We drove in silence through the Lincoln Tunnel under the Hudson River, paid the toll, and zig-zagged through traffic.

"Some guy's on our tail," the driver said. "I'll try to shake him."

By skillful use of the lanes, passing on the inside and the outside, we sped along the freeway and found an open stretch for a mad dash to a sudden cut-off through an exit lane. We stopped at a red light.

"The crapper's been shook," the driver said.

The big man grunted, and we continued along the avenue. About five minutes later the driver cursed.

"A new light's after us," he said.

"It's not the same guy?" the big man said, turning to stare out the back window.

"Oh Christ!" said the third thug.

"The home base's out!" the big man cried. "Drive us the hell out of here!"

The car leaped from a red light and shot into high speed. I knew that they could not risk driving to their rendezvous. The question of my own fate was secondary to theirs. I imagined that it was Storey's gang-mates who had been watching for the license plate which I had had the foresight to give to Storey's thin friend over the telephone. This rival gang was probably closing in for the kill in their home territory of New Jersey. I was too frightened to hope that I was right. The night air whistled by. We must have been doing ninety, I thought. We took a sharp turn and tried to race back for the freeway, but looming ahead, two cars blocked the street. We screeched to a stop, reversed into a turn and began to race back when six headlights stopped in front of us.

"Shall we fire?" the driver asked nervously as he coasted the car to a stop. The headlights almost blinded us.

"We dunno who the hell they are," the big man said. "Wait and see."

"We'd get blasted to hell!" the third thug said, with emphasis on their destination.

"Yeah," the driver whispered. "They got heavy weapons."

I watched figures moving in the dark behind the arcs of the headlights and heard a coarse shout. One of the men called to us to get out with our hands up.

"Geez! I think they're cops!" said the third thug.

"Not a hope," the big man snarled. "Do what they say, and after we learn the score, every guy's on his own." He opened the door, stepped out, reached in to grab me by the wrist and dragged me out.

I put my hands up with my three captors and walked slowly towards what I expected to be new captivity. When we came even with the headlights and stood

94

blinking into the blackness, men began frisking us and taking away small arms. I was roughly pulled to one side. I noticed the spare, silent partner of the late Mr. Storey smile at me.

"Drive this car back into town, Detective."

I was given a little shove, and with a feeling of good will rising out of a constricted stomach, I strode back to the car, saw the keys dangling from the ignition, and waved at the headlights before sitting in the driver's seat. I heard the doors slam, the engines start up, and watched three cars run by me. The cars on the other side had gone in the meantime. I was sitting alone in the stillness on a side road. I was almost afraid to start the engine lest it blow up in my face as an ironic twist to get rid of the evidence. Headlights were approaching in the distance. Fearful of another encounter, I turned on the ignition, spun the steering wheel and headed for the freeway into which the other cars had so recently disappeared.

I followed the directions for Manhattan feeling reasonably certain my criminal friends had gone in the opposite direction. I glanced at the back seat to see that Aragon's case was still there.

So I still had the stamps! I still had my life! But just as important I may have found the best clue yet, the clue that would lead me to the person my kidnappers were taking me to see. That clue was the car I was driving.

TWENTY-ONE

I was awakened by my telephone.

"It's after nine!" Bugofsky cried. "You're late."

"I'm taking sick leave," I mumbled.

There was a pause. "Sick?" Bugofsky said in disbelief. "You're never sick! Get over here, Rudyard. You've got work to do."

"Not today, Bugofsky. You'll see me tomorrow."

"It'll mean your job if you don't get to work," Bugofsky threatened.

I hung up. I was beginning to question Bugofsky's interference. It was as if he was trying to keep me from pursuing the stamp case by making me patrol the Library reading rooms. I thought back to the theft itself. Why had Bugofsky not ordered special security precautions after the first attempt to steal the stamps had been averted? The official excuse was that the work order arranging for the stamps' removal to a safe place had taken longer than expected to be communicated. At the time this seemed reasonable to anyone who knew the slow workings of libraries. But I was suspicious of Bugofsky now.

I called the office of the Manhattan Burglary Squad and reached Detective Buckle. I asked him to check out the serial and license numbers of the car.

"First fingerprints and now license number," Buckle laughed sarcastically. "If you solve this crime, we'll take you on the force."

"I'll think about it," I said.

I left the car in an underground garage because I didn't want to get involved with police in questions about how it came into my possession. My escape from the group who kidnapped me made me a marked man.

While making breakfast, I took New's red stamp album out of my back room and put it in Aragon's case. The two belonged together from now on. Lawyer Harriman was either a fool or a crook for not identifying them correctly. He didn't seem to be a fool.

I took a taxi to Frank Aragon's hotel. No doubt Harriman had informed Aragon that the stamps would have to be returned to him. So I carried the briefcase. I didn't care who had the stamp collection of James New. Aragon had promised to give me the real identity of K. Vanderlyne if he got the stamps back. That name was my price.

Aragon's hotel door had a "Do Not Disturb" sign on the door knob. I knocked loudly. There was no sound. I knocked again and again.

A maid was cleaning the next room. I asked her to open the door. When we entered, we saw Aragon in his pajamas sprawled over his bed. The left side of his head had been blown in. Blood dripped from it onto the rug. The maid, clasping her hands to her face in horror, stood rooted to the floor.

"Don't touch anything," I ordered. I looked at the breakfast tray and saw that the food had not been eaten. Aragon had been duped by the old room service trick. "Go to the next room," I said calmly, "and call management."

As she rushed out, I put my left fist between the mattresses and levered up the top mattress so that I could reach in with my other hand and pull out the red leather stamp album. I put the album in my briefcase and quietly left the room. As I stepped onto the elevator, I realized that the stamps I carried had lost their bargaining power. The only people interested in New's collection would be rich collectors, and now that Aragon, the middleman, was gone, none of them was going to stick his neck out to do a deal for them. In the street, I went to a telephone booth and called Arbie Vine. When her voice came on the line, I took a deep breath.

"Thank God, I caught you," I said. "I'm in trouble."

"Oh dear!" She paused. "What is it? V.D.?"

"Worse than that," I smiled. "I have to know all there is to know about a lawyer called Marshall Harriman from Buffalo as soon as possible."

"I ought to stand idly by and let them kill you," Arbie said angrily. "But since the stamps are public property I want to see them back in the Library."

"Thanks," I said.

"Not for you, Rudy. I'm doing it for the stamps. And I can't guarantee an answer. I'll have to depend on the Bar Association librarians, and they're not in our union."

"I'll call you back late this afternoon," I said and added in a Bogart voice, "Thanks, sweetheart."

"Not funny," she said and hung up.

Like so much of my time on this case, I was waiting for bits of information while others were pressuring me. I was counting on the fact that now Aragon was killed (probably by Storey's friends), there would be no one pressing for my murder. But I could not be certain. At any moment a car could draw up and a handgun could blow me away. Meanwhile, I decided to take a long chance on a hunch. *The International Stamp News* was headquartered on Central Park West within walking distance. I enjoyed a vigorous walk which I had not been getting since I had to rush about in taxis. I found a lean, green-shaded editor in the editorial room of what was a two-roomed establishment. I introduced myself with my New York Public Library detective identification. The editor was surprised and somewhat amused. I told him briefly about my search for the Library's stolen stamps which had caused at least three, maybe more, murders already. The editor looked fascinated.

"One of the unanswered questions can be answered by you," I said.

"I'll do what I can do," the editor said. "Shoot."

I paused for emphasis. "What is the identity of Hippolyte de Leon who writes for you?"

The editor snorted. "How's that going to help?"

"He's involved," I said cryptically.

"Well," the editor sighed, "since you're not with the police or the CIA or the Secret Service, I guess I can tell you." He went to a filing cabinet, took out a sheet of paper, and handed it to me.

At the head of the sheet was typed "de Leon, Hippolyte (Edgar Berney)." There followed Berney's address and a list of articles, the dates they appeared, and the payments made. I was not as surprised as I thought I should have been. I handed back the paper.

"You wouldn't know Kyren Vanderlyne, would you?" I asked.

"A Belgian stamp collector. That's all I know. Why? Was he one of the victims?"

"No, but he might be." I stood up. "Thanks. You can have first crack at the story."

"A bit lurid for us," he said, "but I'll accept it."

I reached Berney's apartment within ten minutes and rang the bell impatiently. Edgar answered the door.

"Mu...mu...Mister Mack," Berney said in surprise.

"Where's your father?" I asked stepping in.

"Shoppin'."

"Seem to be walking all right," I said.

"Oh yeh!. I'm normal al...al...almost," Berney led the way to the living room. "Just as well 'cause I'm getting to the end of di...di...disability." He laughed and sat in an armchair.

I perched on the sofa and leaned forward intently. "I'll come to the point directly. Storey was murdered."

Berney nodded. "Saw it in p...p...papers."

"A stamp collector named Kyren Vanderlyne was involved."

Berney adopted an impassive expression.

"I want to know who he is," I continued. "I think you know."

Berney smiled suddenly. "Yo...yo...you suspect me of everything."

"You've written about his stamp collection, Hippolyte. You ought to know him."

Berney started as if he had been hit by an electric shock.

"By the way," I smiled, "I've got James New's stamp collection in this case." I patted my briefcase. "The same which you accused yourself of stealing."

Berney's adam apple sprang up an down. "I...I...I was kid...kidding."

"I know," I said. "A smart way to sell your stamps for more than they were worth. And they were bought with the Library's expense account. Imagine the chutzpah of misleading the President of the Library to think you had some of the stolen stamps by writing a note under a pseudonym! Hippolyte de Leon!" I shook my head in feigned disapproval. "I've got you on two counts, Edgar. Remember the first? Caught stealing an encyclopedia from the main reading room?"

"Ok...okay," Berney grimaced. "If I tell, you...you...you won't bother me no more?"

"If you tell me everything," I said.

Berney stuck out a long, lean hand and I shook it.

"Harriman," Berney said in one breath. "He's Vanderlyne."

"A lawyer from Buffalo?"

Berney nodded.

Now that I knew, it seemed obvious. It confirmed my suspicion of Harriman's collaboration with Aragon. Since Vanderlyne's fingerprints indicated he took the Inverted Jenny from New's collection, only Harriman could tell me what happened to the stamp.

"You'll be hearing from me, Edgar." I went to the door and let myself out.

At last I had something definite to report to Henry Betterton--evidence that would make him postpone the closing of the case. I stopped at a street phone and called the Library only to find that Betterton could be found in an office on Park Avenue. I took another taxi and remarked at the long column of expenses in my notebook, most of it for taxis.

I found Betterton in a suite of rooms on the third floor of a bank. Betterton, in short sleeves, was distributing papers to some typists. He was surprised by my sudden appearance and seemed uncertain where we should talk. Suddenly he tapped me on the arm as if he had an idea and beckoned me to follow him out of the room down the hallway to a small windowless office which looked as if it had been converted from a cleaning closet.

"All James New's stamps that were stolen are here, with the exception of some sold by a stamp dealer," I said putting the briefcase on the table and opening it. "One important piece is somewhere else where we can get it."

"Good job!" Betterton cried in utter amazement. "Good heavens! I am impressed. What about the Library's stamps?" he asked examining the stamps. "Are they in this group?"

"We have recovered some of them," I said with an undertone of pleasure. "But the Inverted Jenny is key to the remainder."

"Where are those stamps you have recovered?" Betterton asked in amazement.

"In a safe place," I winked and grinned. "There are two groups of organized criminals involved in the case. But I'm going to shock you by saying that Mr. Harriman took the Inverted Jenny."

Betterton looked mystified. "How do you know that?"

"I'll present my evidence after I can prove it."

"Ah huh!" Betterton cried. "Rudy, you're on dangerous ground. You've made a serious accusation against one of the most respected men of the bar in

New York State. Marshall Harriman couldn't possibly be guilty of theft, and certainly not of stealing from one of his clients."

"I think he's the key to breaking the case," I went on undaunted. "He uses a pseudonym, Kyren Vanderlyne. Do you know it?"

Betterton laughed. "No, I don't know it. I think you're making a serious mistake here. Now, I've known Harriman for fifteen years, and he's incapable of dishonesty. Drop this whole line of search." Betterton grew serious suddenly. "The risk is too great for the Library to take. You have to remember that if you are wrong, it is not just a case of your apologizing. You would have brought into question the moral integrity of the Library. Why! it would be a disgrace, and we could never live it down! Our sources of private contribution would dry up!"

"But the trails lead to Harriman," I protested.

"They're false!" Betterton said angrily. "Please, Rudyard, leave Harriman alone and concentrate on finding the real thieves. But good for you that you've recovered the New stamps. I'll return them to Harriman. He'll be pleased."

"I don't think he will be," I said quickly. "He identified some of those stamps as being not from New's collection."

"Did he? Well, perhaps they aren't. I'll take them to the Library tomorrow, and we can try to locate the owner with the help of some experts." Betterton picked up the briefcase and moved for the door.

"Henry," I said. "You will postpone closing the case now, won't you?"

"I'm afraid not," Betterton shook his head. "It seems to me that your investigation is getting farther from the truth, not nearer. Besides, we have to come to terms with the stamps' insurers."

I felt the excitement slip away and looked glumly at Betterton.

"Sorry, Rudyard, I'm advising the trustees tomorrow to write it off as a loss."

We walked down the corridor until Betterton rejoined his secretary-typists busily working on the papers he had given them.

I had been foolish to suggest that my evidence incriminated Harriman. My rashness had cost me victory in the case, lost the stamps for the public, and let Harriman enjoy his successful heist, for I was certain that Harriman was guilty. I lacked solid proof. I did not have the Inverted Jenny itself, after all.

I walked deep in thought along Park Avenue. The giant glass buildings mirrored my feeling of perplexity. I could not put the pieces together properly. If I thought back carefully over all the clues, I should generate enough information to throw a light over my path. I looked at my watch. It was three. I decided I couldn't wait for four to call Arbuthnott. I stepped to the closest street phone.

Arbie answered at the first ring. "You must be telepathic," she said with amusement. "The news on Harriman just came in. There's a lot of it. What do you want?"

"Birthplace and on up," I said.

Arbie sighed. "Here goes. Born Brussels, Belgium."

"Wait," I interrupted. "Was he naturalized?"

"Yes, in 1950, in Buffalo where he got his law degree."

"Did he change his name?"

"Yes, after he was naturalized."

"What name?" I demanded.

"It looks like Kyren Vanderlyne. Am I saying it right?"

My heart jumped. "That's okay. Was that hard to find out?"

"The connection between the names certainly was!" Arbie said. "The archivist in Buffalo said it took him a long time to find it."

"What's Harriman's reputation? Is he respected by judges and fellow lawyers?"

"Oh yeah, a real bourgeois. He fits in with all those crooks like a glove. A real smooth operator."

"Thanks, sweetheart. I'll look at the rest later."

"Wait a minute! Here's a statement in his application to law school: 'I collect stamps.' Isn't that nice? He never mentions it again for the rest of his life."

"Not as Harriman," I added. "He collected under the name of Vanderlyne."

"Rudy. When are we going to see one another?"

"Very soon," I said firmly. "I've got to work non-stop on this case."

"I wish I could believe you." Arbie hung up.

I felt the poignancy in her voice. As an experienced bachelor, I tended to shy away from any hint of claim upon me, but at the same time I was attracted to her vulnerability. There was a crash behind me as two cars collided at an intersection and spun each other round. It brought me back to the real world in which criminals hunted victims in the same violent way. Obviously I now knew too much. If Aragon had given orders to kill me, surely Harriman would too. I decided to appeal to President Stavoris, who was loathe to close the case, and who, as far as I knew, did not know Harriman. It was as if I were appealing for my life. As long as the case stayed open, I could strive to catch the culprit and save myself. As soon as it was closed, I would be a sitting duck waiting to be blasted away at the convenience of the blaster.

TWENTY-TWO

President Stavoris was in his office. He was dictating to a machine follow-up letters to contacts he had made during the day. He had his private ledger open beside him. In it, he assessed how many funds each individual might be persuaded to give to the Library. When I entered, he looked glad to escape from the tedious task for a few moments.

"What's new, Mr. Mack?" He gestured to a chair and pushed his sturdy body back into his own chair as if forcing himself to relax.

"I'm very close to retrieving the Library's stamps." I watched Stavoris's face closely for any tell-tale emotions. "But I'm afraid Mr. Betterton will close the case tomorrow."

"Working on it today, were you?" Stavoris asked. "Mr. Bugofsky said you took sick leave."

I felt guilty.

"Mr. Bugofsky wanted to have you terminated, but I think he was just in another one of his bad moods."

100

"I hope so," I said. "I'd hate to take my discoveries with me."

"Tell me," Stavoris said eagerly. "I need cheering up."

"It's bad news. The man who has our stamps is responsible for Macdonald's death."

Stavoris sat up in astonishment. "Do you mean, his death was not drug-related?"

"You remember I told you that he stole the stamps from the Library when I saw you at the Bettertons' party," I said grimly. "He was working for you, wasn't he?"

"For Continental Insurance which insured the stamps," Stavoris said quickly. "I'm a vice-president and tried to help all I could. Poor John! He was such a determined man. I'm glad he wasn't involved in drugs though." Stavoris still seemed unwilling to acknowledge that Storey had been the stamp thief.

"I know who killed him," I said earnestly.

"You should inform the police!" Stavoris cried.

"But that will lose us the stamps," I said. "What did you do with the stamps you bought from Edgar Berney?"

"Oh those," Stavoris shrugged. "They weren't worth much. Mr. Betterton has them. Why? Berney is not involved is he?"

"Slightly," I smiled. "He is the Hippolyte de Leon you wanted to find."

Stavoris slapped his forehead. "What? Could it be true? Well, I'll be damned! Guess I'm what they call a sucker. Well, that's the end of Mr. Berney."

"Hold on, sir," I said. "I may need him to solve this crime. He's given me the name of the man who I think has the Inverted Jenny: Harriman from Buffalo." I watched to see if the name meant anything to Stavoris. "You don't know him?"

"Never heard of him," Stavoris said.

"He goes also by the name of Vanderlyne."

"Wait! I know that name. My nephew wrote to me from Belgium about him. He was advertising the sale of his stamps, and my nephew asked me to contact him through the Post Office Box number in New York that he gave in his advertisement. My nephew's a bit of a pusher. He wants to get places first," he smiled.

"Probably selling the New stamps abroad," I said aloud.

"What's that?"

"I can do better than a P.O. Box number," I said. "I'll give you his telephone number." I took out my pocket address book, flipped the pages, and jotted down the telephone number on a yellow pad on Stavoris's desk. "Can you arrange to meet with him tomorrow morning and call me tonight to let me know the details? By working together we can bring back the Inverted Jenny," I said with confidence.

"But won't it be dangerous?" Stavoris asked.

I passed off the suggestion with a wave of my hand. Bidding Stavoris good-luck, I left his office, descended to my own and picked up a telephone message from Detective Buckle that my secretary had left in the center of my desk.

"Vehicle owner," it said, "is Salvadore Pappolovecchio, known as 'Papa'. Caution you about deeper involvement."

I sighed with disappointment that the car I drove back in my flight from New Jersey was going to be of no help. Like every other promising clue, it led me in the wrong direction or deeper into the maze. I wondered if Harriman would do the same. My eyes caught the wall clock, and I jumped into action. I had almost forgotten my important appointment.

I opened the door of my apartment to Sybil Betterton. Tall, shapely, and smiling wickedly, she threw her arms about my neck and kissed me long and sensuously.

"Dinner is just about ready. Will you have a drink?" I said, taking her into the sitting room.

"That can wait," she said, pulling me toward the bedroom. "This can't."

"Go ahead," I said pulling my arm away. "I've got to check the kitchen first."

I turned down the burners to a low simmer and felt a low simmer come up in myself. Sybil was voracious. I prepared myself for a love session. Mental preparation was important at my age. I did not want to be overwhelmed. I intended to control this wildcat.

She was standing naked in the bedroom when I stepped in. Her firm uplifted breasts, flat stomach, and long lithesome legs were highlighted by the bed lamp. When I came to her, she began to undress me. Before I could get free of her insistence on denuding me, I found myself on top of her on the bed and working in and out of her to the point where I gained absolute mastery over her. We came together and fell together into a weakness. Sybil was soft, compliant and no longer demandingly aggressive.

I offered her a drink again, and I gave her one of my bathrobes. I went into the kitchen while she prettied herself. I set the table. I had made a chicken curry. Sybil seemed impressed when she ate it. We sat there with the candles, wine, and both of us in bathrobes spontaneously grasping hands across the table.

Sybil talked a bit about herself. Betterton was her third husband. She ventured no information about him which could explain why she was making love with me. She loved traveling; in fact, she drove to all parts of the country on weekends. She knew Europe well, had moved about Asia, been to Africa. She was a restless soul. Her restlessness was in her love-making. When we had finished the strawberries and ice cream and drank the wine to the end, she took me to the sofa and began to caress me. I found myself compelled to return to the bedroom with her. As we fell kissing on the bed together, I asked her if Henry cared.

"He loves me differently," she said, and when I looked mystified, she smiled, "He doesn't like women."

I felt a sudden surge of sympathy for her. I made love to her with renewed desire.

While I was resting my telephone rang. It was William Stavoris who informed me that Harriman was to meet him at the Harvard Club off Fifth Avenue at ten in the morning. I could gain entrance by asking for him.

"That was your friend the Library President," I said.

"He certainly keeps tabs on you," she said.

"We're meeting Marshall Harriman. Do you know him?" I asked innocently.

"Henry often takes him out in the yacht," she said, "but I don't know him very well."

"On his yacht?" My mind began to work. "Does he call it *The Sybil?*" and when she nodded, I asked, "Say, does Henry collect stamps?"

Sybil looked startled. "Not that I know of. He talks a lot about retrieving the Library's stamps."

"Well," I sighed. "It all depends on my meeting with Harriman tomorrow, that is, whether we solve the case."

"Henry said it's hopeless," Sybil smiled. "And Henry is usually right."

At ten past ten the following morning, I gave Stavoris's name to the butler of the Harvard Club and followed him into a sitting room of leather-backed chairs where Stavoris huddled over a coffee table with Harriman. Two packets of stamps were on the table. Harriman appeared to be trying to sell them.

"Mr. Mack, how good of you to join us," Stavoris cried. "I need your advice on this matter of postage stamps."

I admired Stavoris's acting ability. Stavoris was really quite convincing.

Harriman looked as if he wanted to scoop the stamps into his briefcase, and I saw at a glance why he was uncomfortable. Those were the stamps I had turned over to Betterton.

Harriman smiled weakly as I pulled up a chair to inspect the stamps. The trusted family lawyer couldn't lose, I thought. When Aragon failed to deliver the stamps to Harriman's international contact, the stamps were returned to Harriman quite innocently by Betterton. Now Harriman hoped to make a quick sale to Stavoris who would send them abroad to his nephew and thus they'd be buried forever in some kid's stamp collection.

I simply smiled at Harriman and mentioned that Stavoris, as a friend, had asked me to examine the stamps. "They look familiar." I looked quizzically at Harriman.

Harriman cleared his throat. "Indeed, they look somewhat like the stamps you said were stolen from the James New collection. But I assure you they are not. Not the stamps you showed me, and not the stamps from the New collection."

I pulled a sheet of paper from my coat pocket. "I listed details of the stamps when they were in my possession. Would you like to check off these stamps against my list?"

Harriman, taken aback, simply stared at me.

"You will find," I said to Stavoris, "they were the stamps I gave to Mr. Betterton. I received confirmation from James New's son that my descriptive list describes exactly some of the stamps missing from his father's collection." I turned to Harriman. "What do you say to that, Mr. Harriman, considering you are the trustee of the New estate?"

"You're too smart for your own good, Mr. Mack," Harriman hissed.

"Yes," intoned a voice behind us. "I like his smarts." Detective Buckle dropped a newspaper from in front of him and stood up from the easy chair from which he had been listening to the conversation. "I didn't believe that a slick Buffalo lawyer would be dumb enough to sell the stamps from his own client's estate," Buckle intoned. He took the surprised Harriman by the arm, helped him to his feet, and guided him out the door of the sedate club.

Stavoris watched the action with an expression of mild wonderment. "Why didn't you ask him for the Inverted Jenny?" he asked me.

"Because he does not have it," I said. "You might say it has flown to a more secure haven."

"And you know where?" Stavoris's beady eyes lit up in surprise yet expectantly.

"I believe I do, that is, if "batten down the hatches" means what I think it means. It is a phrase of Harriman's," I explained. "I think, at this time, Mr. Edgar Berney is going to repay our kindnesses." I handed the two packets of stamps to the confused Stavoris. "Isn't it just like a city detective to walk off without the evidence? Please bring the stamps I've just given you to the special trustees meeting that Mr. Betterton called for this afternoon."

It suddenly dawned on Stavoris that something dramatic was imminent. He laughed and rubbed his hands. "You mean you're going to reveal the whole truth at that meeting, are you, Rudyard?"

"If we're lucky." I waved to him and headed for the door.

I hired a car on Sixth Avenue and stopped at Berney's apartment. The old man answered the door.

"You again? Why don't you lay off my son?"

"My last request, I promise you," I said pushing by him into the apartment.

Edgar was in the front room planning strategy at the chess board. A slow smile came over his long thin face. "I heard you. Wa...wa...one last favor."

"Right on! Take me to Betterton's yacht."

Berney's smile collapsed. "How do I know wh...wh...where it is?"

"Come here," I grabbed him by the collar of his coat and helped him to his feet. With Berney showing token resistance, I took him by the elbow to the door of his bedroom. "Do you see on the top row of those photographs on the wall? You're leaning over the stern of a yacht with a couple of buddies, right? And on that stern, Edgar, we read *The Sybil*: Betterton's yacht. Now, where the hell is it?"

Berney was looking at his father, who was standing in the hallway behind us, as if asking for guidance.

"Better tell him, son," Berney senior said sadly. "No use gettin' sent up for what the rich folks do. We gotta live." He gave his white goatee a gentle tug.

"Oh...okay," Edgar nodded. "If I show you, ah...ah...are we quits."

"I'll wipe your slate clean, and we'll start again." I gave him a pat on the back.

We drove in silence along the freeway onto Long Island. I could see that Berney was hating himself for the act of betrayal. As for myself, I tried to make sense of the pieces of the puzzle I had put together, but my mind kept refusing to think past the obvious connections. Berney directed me to a marina in a cove along the south shore. The marina watchman knew Berney and let us go by without question. *The Sybil* was one of the larger yachts. Berney led the way up the gangplank. I went immediately into the cabin and looked round at the polished wood furnishings.

"Where are the stamps, Edgar?"

"You just asked me for the ya...ya...yacht," Berney smirked. "Not fair to ask for more."

I noticed the uneven line of the wall bookcase at the back of the cabin. "Never mind." I felt under the shelf at one end of the bookcase and pushed a button. The bookcase turned on an axis and stopped at right angles to allow us access to a small room at the back of it.

"Wow!" Berney cried. "Lu...lucky!"

I regarded him with impatience. "After years of looking for library books hidden in people's apartments, I don't call it luck."

On the walls of the room were large mats of cardboard over which thousands of stamps were arranged by country and date. On the shelf running waist-high around the wall of the room were thousands of stamps strewn loose in disorder. In a small alcove where daylight from an aperture flooded one corner of the room, there was a stand in which were placed two small glass panes and pressed between them a stamp. One of the panes magnified the face of the stamp which was caught in a small mirror placed opposite to it. I saw in the mirror the reflection of a 1918 U.S. 24-cent airmail stamp in which somehow the flying Jenny in the center appeared right-side up within its borders.

The discovery struck me like a revelation. This was the reason for the stamp theft, the murders, and all my weeks of anxiety. Betterton, a sexual invert, had been obsessed with the Inverted Jenny! My God! My mind was making all kinds of connections! By righting the Jenny through the mirror, was he righting himself? I had been right! The motive for the theft was an obsession. All along, I had thought it was a straight-forward collector's obsession. That it was, in addition, Betterton's strange psychological obsession trying to correct his sensual aberration was a revelation to me. How he must have hated his fate! How he must have longed to break out of the shackles of his homosexuality and live a normal life, without pretense, without having to endure the never-ending humiliation of a barren marriage to an attractive, insatiable nymph. The collector's obsession to own the priceless Inverted Jenny, and, by a simple trick of placing the mirror, to be able to see what the stamp would look like right way up must have satisfied his sense of power, where in real life he was powerless. What a twist!

I picked stamp tweezers from the shelf, unscrewed the tiny screw holding the panes of glass together and removed the Inverted Jenny. Carefully putting it in a small envelope, I pocketed it.

"Ever been in here?" I asked.

"Nope," Berney said softly.

I photographed the cabin and the moving bookcase. I snapped a picture of Berney avidly inspecting the stamps.

"Let's go," I said.

"D'rather stay," Berney said.

"Suit yourself." I returned to the car and headed for Manhattan. The thought that Berney would call Betterton crossed my mind, followed by the thought that Betterton's criminal friends might be set in pursuit of me as a consequence, but I dismissed them. Berney was truly interested in stamps.

When I came into Queensborough, I stopped at a telephone booth and called Winslow Margin. I told him to pick up from his safety deposit box the packet of James New stamps and the 1869 U.S. Inverted Centers which belonged to the Library and bring them to the Trustees Room by three.

I was euphoric, relieved and happy now that the resolution of the crime was in sight. But I soon felt a contrary emotion of disappointment and even disillusionment. I had been moving too fast in recent days to give much thought to the philosophical implications of the criminality of trusted members of our society. My old-fashioned values had taken a beating, yet even if Arbie had seen it all from the beginning, I still could not accept her general condemnation of the urbane business class. Maybe my sadness came as much from my acknowledgment that she was right as from my disillusionment with Henry Betterton. I had liked him from the start. He seemed decent, democratic in that I thought he genuinely befriended me, a mere gum-shoe. He never put on airs which I thought was a sure sign of his self-assuredness. He was the kind that our nation entrusts to run things--business, government, institutions. Now I see him as a pitiable creature, humiliated by his wife, a sad man condemned to live a life of lies, and now this: theft, but theft on a grand scale, like a huge avalanche rolling over everything before him, killing, destroying, corrupting all who stood in his way in order to own, possess, dominate what everyone considered priceless and rare.

Being an avid reader of history, I had read of the making and breaking of civilizations. My idea of the world, despite my job of dealing with sordid problems, was nevertheless a bit idealistic. I believed in pillars of society and now I saw my world falling apart. Like empires, the rot destroys from within.

But then suddenly the thought struck me that I was thinking like the conservative-minded hetrosexual that Arbie had called me. Could not Betterton have seen his sexual preference as normal and righted the stamp's inverted center as an act of justification, as a humorous, somewhat ironical gesture in homage to the absurdity of life? I laughed aloud at the possibility that both interpretations could be correct and yet be so adversarial that the balancing of them in my mind seemed comical. Maybe our civilization was not falling apart but evolving into something new.

By the time I returned my rented car and entered the Library, I had barely one hour to prepare for the trustees meeting. I found a cryptic message, left in the neat hand of my secretary who had not yet returned from lunch, from Arbuthnott: "Buy-and-Cadge-It retail chain--Bankrupt." I blessed Arbie for her perseverance in digging up this important bit of information. It could well lead me to a motive for the theft. I went immediately to the Economics Division and consulted company directories and the latest periodical indices. When I found what I had to know, I just had time to pick up the last two volumes of *Baker's Encyclopedia* from the General Research Reading Room shelves, some paraphernalia from my office, and enter the Trustees Room before the guards locked the doors to the meeting. I sat in a chair against the wall and watched Stavoris call the meeting to order.

Stavoris explained that the special meeting was called to deal with particular problems, the first of which was the stamp theft. He apologized for the fact that Henry Betterton seemed to be late, but he called on Rudyard Mack for enlightenment in the case.

I experienced a tightening of my nerve ends and a weakness in my stomach. I reached the head of the table and found my voice with difficulty. "Ladies and Gentlemen. We have recovered the stamps that were stolen from the Library," was all I could blurt out. In the ensuing expressions of surprise and delight, I took from my briefcase the Postmaster Provisionals. I held them up and explained, "The complete two blocks--one of ten and one of nine--were located in the lining of the inside covers of the two encyclopedia volumes I have placed on the table. I shall pass one volume to my left, the other to my right and ask you to inspect the incisions in them into which the stamps were hidden. Actually, the stamps were taken by a Mr. Storey in the early hours of the morning before the theft was detected. The man whom I shall identify only as Mr. X had made it possible for Storey to do so from Mr. X's familiarity with the security guards' round of inspection. Once Storey lifted the stamps from the display cases, he took them into the Allen Room next to the stamp display by means of a key furnished to him by Mr. X. Once in the Allen Room, Mr. Storey put the stamps into the incisions in the covers of twelve volumes of the encyclopedia delivered to one of the readers' cubicles. Mr. Storey then hid in the Allen Room. When the Library opened to the public, Mr. Storey simply left the Allen Room and passed easily out of the Library. He intended to return to retrieve the stamps from the encyclopedia volumes but because they were a reference work from the open shelves of the Reading Room and were only allowed to be removed by special permission of the Chief of the Division for a short time, Mr. Storey discovered that they had gone back to the shelves by the time he returned to the Allen Room. Storey notified Mr. X who then arranged with a co-conspirator staff-member to smuggle the encyclopedia volumes from the reading rooms out of the Library's stack windows in the dead of night and leave them in a locker at Grand Central Station for Mr. Storey."

I saw that the trustees were fascinated. I took a sip of water from a glass on the table. "Ten volumes were successfully removed in this way. In the remaining two, which I retrieved, I shall not say how for the moment, I found the Postmaster Provisionals. In the ten volumes were the 1909 U.S. "Star Plates" in four blocks and the 1869 Inverted Centers. Mr. Storey took the stamps from these volumes from the locker in Grand Central Station and delivered them to Mr. New in Buffalo, the full story of which will follow. I am glad to say, to cut the long story short, that all of these stamps have been recovered by the distinguished stamp dealer sitting in the audience, Mr. Winslow Margin." I beckoned to Winslow who glided forward and laid the stamps out on the table as I continued. "As a dealer, he sold stamps which came from a reputed international stamp organization based in Brussels but which became defunct years ago and whose name was assumed by Mr. X as a front for his business of selling stolen stamps. Mr. Margin, through our counsel, elicited all of these

107

stamps from this front organization of Mr. X under the pretense of having found a buyer for them. The stamps before you represent 154 of the 155 missing. The remaining stamp," I reached into my breast pocket, took the stamp out of the envelope and held it up between my fingers, "the Inverted Jenny was held by Mr. X." I took another sip of water to see the effect on the trustees. They sat still and looked intently at me. I continued, "It was in the possession of Mr. James New of Buffalo who had arranged the theft of the stamps with Mr. X, but through Mr. New's indiscretion of boasting of his possession of it, he was killed. This led to a series of murders by crime figures linked to a Buffalo crime family and to a rival crime family from New Jersey to which the late Mr. Storey belonged. Mr. Storey alias Mr. Macdonald of the Continental Insurance Company successfully retrieved the stamps from the Grand Central locker, you will recall, and delivered them to Mr. New. When Mr. New was murdered, Storey was misled by Mr. X to believe that James New had been killed by unknown persons and that New's stamps were being sold secretly by Winslow Margin. Mr. X deliberately tried to throw all suspicion off himself and off his partners in theft, Mr. Harriman and Mr. Aragon, both of Buffalo. I must say, he threw me off the scent too. Our President Stavoris was also misled by his information." Stavoris smiled sheepishly as I took a sip of water and continued. "The gory details of the crime you will, of course, read in the newspapers." I caught the eye of the editor of the *International Stamp News* who was in the audience and taking notes. "For his important help in finding the stamps, I wish to publicly thank Edgar Berney of the Science Division." A guard stepped up and whispered in my ear that there was an urgent telephone call for me. I excused myself and said, "Perhaps Mr. Stavoris will acquaint you with the fate of Mr. Harriman while I answer a telephone call." I stepped to a table at the side of the room as Stavoris carried on. The voice on the phone belonged to Sybil Betterton.

"I'm at Henry's marina," she announced. "Henry's killed himself." She cut me short from speaking. "He stayed at home this morning and told me he was going to drop in here on his way to the trustees' meeting. He found Edgar Berney who told him what you'd done. He stared at himself in a small mirror for about five minutes, told Edgar to get off the ship, and bang! Edgar heard a shot shortly afterwards." There was a long silence.

"I'm sorry," I said.

She began talking again. "He was tired with the obsession of living upright," Sybil sounded resentful. "You shouldn't have done this, Rudy. I won't see you again."

"Let's talk about it," I said.

"No. I'm finished with you. You amused me while I had Henry. Now I shall have to look for another rich husband," she said, rather viciously and hung up.

I shrugged and returned to the trustees. Stavoris was just ending his account of Harriman's role in selling the stamps. I took over the floor and said, "I have only to add," I cleared my throat, "that I suppose the theft took place in the first place because Mr. New and his partner needed money to finance a failing retail chain, "Buy-and-Cadge-It." I noticed a thin young man leave the audience to give

108

a sheet of paper to a guard who brought it to Stavoris. "There may have been other reasons, of course," I added.

A lady trustee from one of the nation's richest families interrupted me. "Tell me, Mr. Mack, who is this Mr. X you refer to?"

"Mr. X?" I repeated and paused. "Why, he was the Inverted Jenny," I smiled.

Stavoris chuckled and stood up. He took over from me and said, "Mr. Mack is not permitted to say who Mr. X is, at the moment, until legal proceedings can be under way. He's entitled to keep some secrets after all. Now, for other news, I have just received a note from the son of James New who is here today. I would like to share with you what his note says. He's donating the stamp collection of his father, which I understand has just been recovered, to the Library to be shown with the Miller Collection. His family hopes that it atones for his father's mistakes."

I caught Sharkey Bugofsky's look of absolute dismay as Sharkey stood listening from the entrance to the Executive Offices. For security reasons, he had hoped the stamps were lost forever. I doubted that the stamps would be exhibited for a long time.

As Stavoris closed the meeting, I felt a tug at my sleeve. Arbie Vine looked up at me.

"Free for dinner tonight?"

"I am," I smiled and put my arm about her shoulders as if to say I was ready to fraternize with the union president anywhere.

"Why the praise of Berney?" Arbie asked.

"Keeping my word," I whispered. "I expect him to keep his word to stay clean. Say," I cried happily, "let's join Sharkey for a drink. It's time he congratulated me for doing something right."